MR. RIGHT AGAIN FOR HER

COWBOY CONFESSIONS, BOOK #4

JO GRAFFORD

Mr. Right Again for Her

Cover design: Jo Grafford of JG PRESS

ISBN: 978-1-63907-048-0

ACKNOWLEDGMENTS

Many thanks to my editor, Cathleen Weaver, for helping make this story the best it can be. I also appreciate my amazing beta readers — Debbie Turner, Mahasani, and Pigchevy. I want to give another shout out to my Cuppa Jo Readers on Facebook. Thank you for reading and loving my books!

CHAPTER 1: TWIN TROUBLE

DEVLIN

"Whoa! Watch where you're going, bro!" Devlin Cassidy had to perform a rapid two-step to dance out of his twin brother's way.

"Can't." Emerson's voice was muffled from the other side of the boxes he was busy lugging from the storage room. They were stacked so tall that he couldn't see over the top of them.

"Any reason you're not using the dolly this morning?" Devlin called irritably after him. "You know... like we always do?" He watched his brother slowly make his way toward the main display rack at the front of their family's store. His blonde hair dragged the collar of his polo shirt. Like his twin, he wore his hair on the longer and tousled side, though his face was clean shaven.

"Yeah. This is a better workout." Emerson set the tall stack on the counter by the cash register. Then he turned to give his twin a mocking grin as he flexed his biceps and blew on them. "I don't mind co-managing this place, but I have no intention of letting my pipes turn into spaghetti noodles in the process."

He was in an evergreen polo this morning with the Cassidy Farm logo emblazoned across the pocket — a horse's head with a flowing mane surrounded by a wreath of corn stalks. The shirt boasted ribbed short sleeves that showed off his farmer's tan. Every guy in their family had sun-kissed faces and hands from the number of hours they spent outdoors.

"Good to know." Devlin folded his arms and watched in amusement as Emerson produced a box cutter from the back pocket of his jeans. He figured there was more to the story, since his brother was constantly lifting weights to stay in shape. The cabin they shared was littered with the bars, free weights, and protein drink mixes to prove it. However, he also knew his twin wouldn't spill the beans about whatever was bothering him until he was good and ready.

Emerson shoved his Stetson farther back on his head as he removed the top box from his stack, slapped it on the cabinet, and sliced it open with a flourish. Then he started pulling out jars, packages, and trial-sized tubes of their mother's line of hand-crafted personal care products. There was hand lotion, liquid soap, bar soap, body wash, shampoo, bath bombs, candles, facial treatments, moisturizers, makeup removers, and lip balm — all made with the pure, organic honey collected from her prized bee farm.

He waited until he emptied the first box before

glancing up and sniping, "Are you going to just stand there and watch?"

"Oh. My bad!" Devlin uncurled his arms and swaggered slowly in his twin's direction. "Didn't want to horn in on your landmark body building session there."

"Very funny."

"So, what are we lifting this morning? Ah. Body wash." He grabbed two bottles of it and did a few arm curls with them. "Good workout, bro! A few hundred more reps, and I might actually start feeling the burn," he teased.

"Eh, put a plug in it, will ya?" Emerson gave him a not-so-gentle bump with his shoulder.

Devlin shoulder-bumped him back. "Who is she?" The only other time he'd seen his brother so disgruntled, a woman had been involved.

"Don't know what you're talking about." Emerson's voice was terse.

"If you say so." Dev didn't believe him for a second. A twin instinctively knew when his twin was lying. "Just for the record, getting to help run the family business with you is the biggest honor." He shot his brother a curious look. "Even on the days you're mad at me." He doubted most people enjoyed what they did for a living half as much as he did.

Emerson shot him a glum look. "I'm not mad at you."

"Could've fooled me." Dev knew if he poked at his brother long enough, he'd eventually poke back.

They worked in silence for a few minutes, swiftly

emptying the stack of boxes. Devlin studied the fully stocked display rack with satisfaction, knowing the honey products would start flying off the shelves the moment the store opened. He was proud of his mother for coming up with such a genius idea. He was also proud of his oldest brother and ranch manager, Asher, for working so hard to market their proprietary line of products. He was forever securing new billboards, talk show interviews, and ad space on websites to keep Cassidy Farm front and center in the hearts and minds of their customers.

"Do you ever miss the rodeo circuit?" Emerson abruptly paused in the middle of breaking down boxes to face his twin.

"Sometimes, I guess." Dev shrugged, feeling his insides turn cold. "Why do you ask?" It was a sore topic with him, and his twin knew it. It seemed kind of cruel to bring it up today of all days. Just thinking about Julia Benson made him press the heel of his hand to his chest. She'd dumped him eight long and lousy years ago to pursue a rodeo career.

And now she was back in town.

"Because I miss it sometimes, too." Emerson grimaced and spread his hands. "The buck of a wild bronc beneath me, the burn of the wind in my face, the roar of the crowd—" He broke off suddenly, staring hard at his brother. "Aw, snap! Wasn't thinking about how all that would sound to you. I didn't mean—"

"I know you didn't." Dev had no interest in going there. It wasn't his brother's fault that Julia had ended things between them when he'd chosen not to join her on the rodeo circuit. They'd only been eighteen-years-old at the time and fresh out of high school — full of impossible dreams and a thousand shades of other nonsense — all of which had come to a screeching halt the day his grandfather had passed away.

Overnight, the burden of running Cassidy Farm had fallen on his parents, him, and all five of his brothers. He'd tried to keep Julia in town by proposing marriage to her, but that hadn't worked, either. It was way too soon in their relationship to pop such a question. She'd turned him down flat, of course. Unfortunately, it was something his heart had never gotten over.

His gaze narrowed on his twin. "You *did* mean what you said about missing the old days, though. The question is why. Why now?" He waved vaguely to take in the spacious Cassidy Farm store. "Things are going good for us again." They got to work alongside the people they loved and trusted the most. They got to raise and sell their own beef, fresh produce, and honey products. They got to be their own bosses, and they made good money doing it.

Emerson glanced away. "Is there any chance you'll forget we had this conversation?"

Dev snorted. "Not likely, but I can take a hint. You don't want to talk about it, so we won't."

"Not talking about stuff seems to be our new norm, huh?"

Dev stiffened at the argumentative note in his brother's voice. "Now, what?"

"You have to ask?" Emerson's sigh was long and loud as he made a few more slashing movements with his box cutter. The cardboard boxes collapsed, one by one, into a neat stack. "Fine! I'll just say it. You haven't been yourself since Julia Benson blew back into town.

"It's complicated." Dev raised his hands in warning. His ex was the last thing he wanted to talk about.

"You can say that again," his twin chortled. "At least half the town saw her plant one on you at the kissing booth last weekend."

Dev felt his face heat with a mixture of anger and hurt at the reminder that a whole week had passed since the annual hoedown. Another whole week in which Julia had yet to make up her mind if she wanted the clean break they'd never officially given each other eight years ago. It was beginning to look like she was up to the same old tricks. The same old head games. The same old stringing him along. He couldn't believe he'd fallen for it a second time.

"Store's about to open in five," he growled, hating how much of a fool she was making of him all over again. "Time to get our game faces on."

"I was born with my game face on, bro." With an unholy grin, Emerson swept the collapsed boxes off the cabinet and marched with them in the direction of the back storage room. "You're the one who'd better slap one on nice and quick, seeing who's about to be our first customer of the day." Without turning around, he jammed his thumb toward the glass double doors.

Whatever. Shaking his head in derision, Dev strode toward the entrance to flip their CLOSED sign around to OPEN.

And stopped short.

Julia Benson was standing on the other side of the glass, impatiently tapping the toe of one custom tooled cowgirl boot. At the sight of him, she shoved a handful of her long blonde hair over her shoulder and lifted her chin defiantly.

His heart sank at the undeniable pout twisting her full lower lip. Unsure if he had enough fight in him for a confrontation with her this morning, he dragged in a bracing breath and took his time unlocking the doors. *God, give me strength.*

The kiss she'd planted on him last Saturday at the 2nd Annual Chipper Hoedown was still burning his mouth and scalding his heart. Yeah, the hundred dollars she'd spent on it was for a good cause — to help fund the new elementary school playground. Still, she could've kissed any of the guys manning the stalls that day. Why had she marched up to him? From what he could gather, he was the only guy she'd kissed, too. It had been eight years since the last time they'd kissed. Eight stinking, long, gut-wrenching years, yet she'd still had the ability to turn his heart inside out and upside-down after all this time.

I'm just pitiful, apparently. Or cursed. Not that Dev would've admitted it to anyone, but she'd ruined him for any other woman. He'd spent the last eight years rarely dating. And the few dates he'd been on, he'd managed to torture himself the entire evening by mentally comparing everything they said or did to the way Julia said and did stuff. And all his other dates had come up painfully short. *Because I'm that pitiful.*

Giving the lock a vicious twist with his Allen wrench, he pushed open the door for her. "Welcome to Cassidy Farm," he intoned blandly, the same way he would greet any other customer. Well, that wasn't exactly true. He'd have been a lot nicer if it was anyone else but her. He wondered what she was doing here and feared he was about to find out.

She looked good, *really* good, as she breezed past him smelling like honey shampoo and hand lotion — the kind they sold right here in his family store. Her jeans had a sassy red rose embroidered on the hip, and the denim flared out at the ankles over her boots. Her freshly pressed red and white checkered shirt was tucked into the waist of her jeans and anchored there with a gem-encrusted silver belt. She looked every inch the rodeo queen and barrel racing champion that she was. Her success had come at a steep cost, though. She'd chosen her career over him.

It still hurt.

Twirling his way, she took a swaying step backward, then another, silently beckoning him to follow her. "Can we talk? About...you know...about the other day?" From the look on her face, she was every bit as troubled as he was about what had happened between them.

However, he was in no mood to give her the satisfaction of knowing that she'd gotten that far under his skin. Again. Instead, he shrugged and strove to adopt a casual tone. "Isn't that what we're doing?" Fury prickled through his veins over the fact that she'd taken a full week and change to come looking for him after their last conversation. Man, but he was sick to death of the way she toyed with his feelings. He was getting too old for stuff like that. They both were.

"Alone." She glanced around them.

His heart thumped at the realization she was finally ready to deal with the consequences of the kiss they'd shared. Either that, or she was finally ready to break things off with him for good, and he still wasn't ready for that. *So blasted pitiful!* He knew it was cowardly of him to avoid the inevitable, but he found himself mentally scrambling for a way to end their conversation before their final breakup could take place.

He searched her gaze for any clue as to what was really on her mind, but her shuttered eyes and pale features gave away nothing. "You're the only customer in the store," he pointed out coolly.

A red spot appeared in the middle of each cheek. "What about your brother?" she hissed, darting another furtive look around them.

His anger percolated a few degrees higher. "He's not a customer."

"Please, Dev." Julia's voice swelled with so much wistfulness that it twisted his insides.

Knowing she didn't deserve his sympathy, he hardened his heart against the sound. Before he could formulate his next comeback, the front doors jingled with another customer.

He pressed a hand to his chest, feigning regret. "Sorry. Duty calls."

"Dev," she pleaded as he pivoted away from her.

He shrugged again. "If you want to stick around, I'll see what I can do when Emerson returns." He knew he was being a jerk, but he was too angry to rein in his temper at the moment. How dare she march into his place of employment on a Monday morning, expecting him to drop everything for her drama! She could've gotten ahold of him anytime throughout the weekend. If she'd forgotten his work hours, which he sorely doubted was the case, she could've easily checked the sign on the front door.

Cassidy Farm closed mid afternoon on Saturdays and was closed all day on Sundays every week of the year. It had been like that since they'd first opened their doors. A few folks complained about their limited weekend hours, but his family had managed to run a profitable business despite it. It pretty much guaranteed their store was packed to overflowing on Saturday mornings.

"I'll stay," Julia muttered behind his back.

He didn't acknowledge that he'd heard her.

A trio of white-headed ladies puttered across the

entrance mat to the row of carts just inside the door. It was the Mullins sisters. Two were widows, and one was a spinster. After years of living apart from coast to coast, they'd finally reunited last year in Chipper, of all places.

Dev had no idea why they'd chosen his small hometown. At the moment, he was simply glad they were on their normal schedule. They showed up every Monday morning to purchase their weekly supply of meat and fresh produce.

Instead of grabbing a cart, all three of them looped the handle of a basket over their wrists. They never purchased large quantities of anything, preferring to putter through the store and purchase bits of this and that.

"Morning, Dev!" the oldest one called to him.

"Morning, Francine," he called back, tipping his Stetson at her. He adored the way they dressed up to come shopping. All three women were sporting pantsuits, low-heeled pumps, and way too much makeup. He'd always suspected that their visit to Cassidy Farm was one of their biggest outings of the week.

The youngest sister, Prim, gave a breathless titter as she smiled at him. She was the one who'd never married. "Mercy," she announced to her sisters in a voice intended for him to hear. "What's wrong with these local gals? Allowing any of the Cassidy boys to remain single should be considered a crime. Arrest them all, I say!" She shot a mischievous look around the store, very likely in search of Emerson, whom she liked to tease just as mercilessly about his single state.

By her arrested look and parted red lips, Dev perceived she'd caught sight of someone else entirely. "Oh, dear!" She dipped her head closer to her sisters. Whatever she said this time was too low for him to hear.

Emerson appeared at Dev's elbow. "I got this," he assured with a snicker. "You can go deal with your woman now."

"Nah, that's okay." Dev squared his shoulders. "I'll take care of the Mullins sisters. I've already gotten started with them."

"Really?" Emerson rocked back on the heels of his boots, raising his eyebrows in challenge. "You wouldn't, by any chance, be avoiding—"

"I said I've got this," Dev snarled. Without waiting for his twin to answer, he strode up to the three sisters. "Have y'all sampled any of Mom's autumn scented lotions yet?"

Prim indulged him with another red-lipped smile. She'd colored a little out of the lines at the corners, giving her mouth a slightly clownish appearance. "Only the honey pumpkin one, love. What else has that sweet mama of yours stirred up?"

"I'm glad you asked." He lightly slid an arm around her shoulders as he steered her toward the display rack he and Emerson had just finished stocking. "She's bottled two more since last week — honey apple and honey berry."

Prim's smile widened. "I'll take one of each."

He cocked his head at her. "Don't you want to try a sample first?"

"No. I'd rather be surprised when I get home." She angled her head at him. "Everything Claire Cassidy creates is divine, and I mean everything!" She allowed her gaze to drop to his boots and slowly work their way up his tall frame. Long before her gaze reached his face, she'd burst into another girlish giggle.

———

From her perch on a stool in the Cassidy Farm Bakery, Julia watched the elderly women flirt with her ex. Never before had she encountered a more shameless bunch. All three of them looked old enough to be his grandmother, for pity's sake!

Fuming with jealousy at his insistence on paying attention to them instead of her, she plopped her elbows on the table in front of her and rested her chin in her hands. Good golly, but she wanted to wring Dev's neck for making her wait like this! It had seriously taken her an entire week to work up the courage to face him again. She'd been losing sleep, having trouble eating, the whole enchilada. Coming here was the hardest thing she'd ever done. Harder than any rodeo she'd ever ridden in. Harder than any buckles she'd risked life and limb to earn.

And now he was avoiding her. Or punishing her. She wasn't sure which. All she knew was that he hadn't been the least bit welcoming when she walked through the door this morning. Which was pretty unbelievable, considering the kiss they'd shared a little over a week ago.

Yeah, the tension and attraction was still very much radiating between them, but there was anger in him, too. And resentment. It was rolling off of him thicker than butter.

"Yo!"

She jolted at the sound of Emerson's voice, then scowled up at him for startling her. She hadn't heard him approach. Knowing him, he'd probably snuck up behind her on purpose, just to be annoying.

"You scared me," she muttered, a little ashamed of herself for not paying more attention to his whereabouts.

"Clearly." He slapped his palms down on the table. "What can I getcha? Coffee? Donuts?"

"Your brother," she snapped without thinking, then immediately blushed. "I came to speak to Dev," she explained in a rush. "Never dreamed he'd be so busy the moment the store opened." She didn't bother hiding her sarcasm.

The door jingled every few minutes with yet another incoming customer, so she knew her window of opportunity to speak with him was fast disappearing. That's why she'd shown up the moment the store opened.

Emerson scowled at her. "A word of advice."

She lifted her chin. "I didn't come here looking for advice."

He leaned closer to her. "Don't worry. It's free."

"Oh, goody!" She rolled her eyes at him, mentally congratulating herself for keeping her voice light. It was a good thing he couldn't see how shaky her insides were.

"From my angle, you've spent the past eight years giving your blasted horses more time and attention than you ever gave my brother back when you were dating."

Her lips parted in a gasp of protest. "That's not fair!"

"Am I wrong?" He arched a single blonde eyebrow at her.

She stared at him in consternation. "It takes two to fight. You can't put all that on me."

"Maybe not, but you're the one who walked away."

She shook her head in disbelief at him. "I was an eighteen-year-old pursuing a lifelong dream. There's no crime in that!" Was he entirely forgetting the part about how she and Dev were supposed to pursue that dream together? As far as she was concerned, he was the one who'd failed to hold up his end of the bargain.

"You broke his heart," Emerson muttered, glancing away.

"He broke mine first," she stormed. "He was supposed to come with me, you know."

"He planned to, right up to the point when Grandpop died."

She nodded, her eyes growing damp. "He was a good man. I'm sorry you lost him so soon."

"You should have stuck around longer," Emerson pressed, searching her features so pointedly that she shuddered.

She blinked back tears. "I couldn't." That was yet another one of the things she'd finally worked up the courage to confess to Dev this morning. She shot an anxious look in his direction and found him still hovering over the Mullins sisters. She'd never seen him so ridiculously attentive to a set of customers before. Her gut told her he was only doing it to avoid her.

Emerson jutted his chin at her, reclaiming her attention. "Why not?"

She pressed her lips together, debating how truthful she wanted to be with him. She would've preferred to tell Dev first. "Things were bad at home."

"What do you mean by bad?" His blonde brows drew together in concern.

She blew out a breath, lifting her bangs momentarily from her forehead as she straightened on the stool. "To say that my stepmom and I didn't get along back then is a royal understatement. We fought like cats and dogs. Our last argument before I left home was so ugly that Dad threatened to disown me." It had been about Dev, of course. Tonna Benson had been fit to be tied over the fact that her stepdaughter hadn't said yes when he'd proposed.

Emerson's frown deepened. "I would've never guessed that. Y'all sure put on a good act in public."

She sniffed. "You can thank my dad for that. He

threatened to take my truck keys away on a regular basis for my failure to accept her as my mother. As if you can just demand something like that!" She wrinkled her nose at the memory. "But you can't. I could barely tolerate being in the same room with that woman!"

Julia hadn't realized she was clenching and unclenching her fists on the table until Emerson reached over to blanket her hands with one of his.

"I had no idea things were that rough between you and your stepmom. Dev never said anything about it."

"He didn't know."

"Why not?"

"I didn't want his sympathy or anyone else's. I just wanted to get away from it all." Which she'd done, with no thought of how steep the cost would be in the long run. She caught her lower lip between her teeth to keep it from trembling.

Emerson nodded gravely, absorbing everything she'd told him. "What made you come back, Jules?"

She stared at their joined hands, wondering if he'd meant for the endearment to slip out. No one but the Cassidy brothers had ever called her that. "My dad is sick," she sighed. "And since my stepmom is no longer here, there's no one but me to look after him." Tonna Benson had lost her battle with breast cancer a couple of years ago. Her father had yet to recover from it. He'd been on a downward spiral ever since.

"Will you bite my head off if I say I'm sorry for your loss?" Emerson squeezed her hand.

"No." Julia sniffed. "She and I finally made our peace a while back."

"I'm glad."

"Me, too. I've got enough things to feel guilty about without having that on my shoulders, too," she admitted wryly.

"Oh?" His gaze narrowed on hers. "Anything I can help out with before you take off?"

"Now that you mention it," she made a face at his not-so-subtle attempt to get her to open up further. "Do you sell anything at Cassidy Farm for sore muscles?" She hoped he wouldn't ask why, because she really didn't want to discuss her career-ending injury. Or admit that a former champion barrel racer had re-injured herself last week while serving as a team mom for Cormac Cassidy's Little League team. In her anxiety to work her way back into the Cassidy brothers' good graces, she'd spread herself a little too thin lately, and now she was paying the price for it.

"Sure do." He snorted. "Dare I ask who's injured?"

"No, you may not!" They became locked in a brief staring contest.

It ended with him squaring his broad shoulders and straightening to his full height. "Follow me." Keeping a hand under her elbow, he led her to the same display rack at the front of the store where Dev was standing with the Mullins sisters.

Dev shot a dark look in their direction. His gaze

lingered for a moment on the hand his brother had beneath her elbow. Then he angled his head at the Mullins sisters, urging them toward the produce section of the store.

Julia stared after them, aghast at how blatantly he was avoiding her. He wasn't even trying to hide it. That hurt.

She barely listened as Emerson sold her a whole bag of his mom's signature honey products — everything from lotion for her chapped fingers to a herbal wrap for her sore knee.

"Good grief, Julia!" His exasperated voice finally drew her back to the present. "I feel like I'm taking advantage of you."

"Why?" She blinked in confusion at him.

"Because you keep nodding at everything I'm throwing in your shopping bag."

"So? I can afford it."

"Just look inside the bag and tell me if you actually want any of this stuff."

"I'm sure it's fine." She shook her head, feeling sad. "Just ring it up already. I've gotta get back to my dad. Tell Dev I'm sorry I couldn't wait any longer. If he ever finds the time to talk, he's got my number."

Emerson moved items across the scanner in silence. Only when he finished bagging her purchases did he speak again. "He was hurt really bad when you left, and he's hurting again now that you're back."

I know the feeling. "I'm sorry," she whispered raggedly.

"Have you told him that?" he asked quietly.

"Maybe I was waiting for him to say it first." She lifted her chin. "He's not the only one who got hurt. Planes fly in both directions," she reminded tightly. "Phones ring in both directions, too."

"Maybe he didn't think you wanted to hear from him."

"Maybe he was wrong." She blindly snatched up her bag and headed for the door.

"Talk is cheap," he called in a low voice. "Maybe you should do something to show him you still care."

She paused at the door, shoulders sagging. Her leg was aching nearly as badly as her heart. *I think it's too late.* If there was any truth to the rumors flying around about Dev Cassidy and Rosie McKeever, then Julia was most definitely too late. It was no wonder he was giving her such a cold shoulder this morning.

She pushed open the door and left the store without looking back.

CHAPTER 2: MISSING HORSE
DEVLIN

Though he tried to ignore her, Dev was very aware of Julia's every movement. The jingle of the doorbell as it shut behind her resounded through his chest like a death knell. He cut off his conversation with the Mullins sisters in mid-sentence. "If you'll excuse me, ladies, I need to handle something up front."

Amidst a volley of knowing smiles and chuckles, they assured him they could finish their shopping without his assistance — that he'd already been so very helpful.

He stomped over to the checkout counter, where Emerson was idly straightening a stack of shopping baskets. "You and Julia seemed mighty cozy during her visit."

"I guess." Emerson didn't immediately look up. "In case you've forgotten, Jules used to be like family to all of us, bro."

"Past tense," Dev snarled. "And don't call her that."

"Dude! Get a grip." Emerson's head came up. He stared at his brother in consternation. "She's still a customer, not to mention the daughter of one of Chipper's founding families. You'd be wise to keep the peace with her."

"Or what?" Dev grated out. He knew he was being unfair, unreasonable, and everything in between. However, seeing Julia snuggle up to another one of his brothers in the space of a few weeks had been almost more than he could bear. First, serving as Cormac's team mom, and now holding hands with his twin. Why couldn't she just leave well enough alone?

"Or," Emerson gave him a hard look, "a certain sister-in-law might shoot us both if we do anything to cause Julia Benson's father to withdraw his pledge to help build the elementary school playground."

Dev continued glaring at him, feeling trapped.

"For what it's worth, I hear he's been pretty sick."

"I take it we're still referring to Cody Benson?"

"Who else?"

"Man!" Dev lifted his Stetson to drag his fingers through his hair. "I hadn't heard."

"Doesn't sound like he's told many folks. He's been pretty reclusive, come to think of it, since his wife died."

I wouldn't know, since I've been avoiding the Bensons altogether for years. Another thought struck Dev. "Is he the real reason Julia's back in town?" He clapped his hat back on his head.

"I don't know." Emerson looked exasperated. "Maybe you should ask her. You know, instead of avoiding her like you did the past half hour." He held up a hand when his twin started to splutter. "Don't bother denying it. We both know I could've stepped in at any point to help the Mullins sisters."

"That shoe's on the other foot," Dev grumbled. "She's been avoiding me since the hoedown." He couldn't believe they'd shared such an explosive kiss, and all he'd gotten from her afterward was crickets.

"And you returned the favor in spades this morning."

"Can't believe she expected me to drop everything on the job for a conversation that can only take place in private." No way was he allowing her to drag his name through a public breakup and all the humiliation that came with it.

"Why's that?" Emerson studied him curiously.

"At the hoedown, she claimed we never officially broke up." Feeling like his chest was about to explode, Dev pressed a hand to his heart.

"What?" His brother's voice rose to a near shout, making the Mullins sisters spin in their direction. He quickly lowered his voice. "Holy smokes, Dev! Are you saying you two are still dating?"

"No way! Of course not!"

"But you just said…" His brother's voice rose again.

"I only repeated what she said, and I'd appreciate you keeping your voice down."

"I'm trying. It's just—" Emerson bumped into the baskets, nearly knocking them over. He made a dive for the stack, catching them in the nick of time.

"Julia and I are not dating," Dev growled in undertones. "I just didn't want a public breakup, okay?"

"You really sure that's what she planned on doing?" Emerson looked so incredulous that a thread of cautious hope wound its way through Dev's chest. "I mean, she made it sound to me like she just wanted to talk."

"Yeah, well, we're done talking." Dev knew he sounded petty, but his heart was too raw to be reasonable at the moment. Talking with Julia Benson hurt too much.

"Not if you're still dating, bro." Emerson snorted out a laugh. "I've never met a woman who's done talking with her man."

"I'm not her man."

"Uh, sounds to me like you are." Emerson's blonde eyebrows rose in a challenge.

Dev let out a frustrated huff of air. "We took an eight-year break from each other. No one in their right mind would consider us still together." The fact that Julia was pretending otherwise was downright cruel. It was like she was determined to break his heart all over again.

"You took a break, huh?" Emerson leaned back against the far cabinet, folding his arms. "So, she's not wrong. You two never officially ended things, which means—"

"We're not together," Dev snarled. His stupidly weak heart would give anything for another chance with her, but he was pretty sure that wasn't what his ex had in mind. *Shoot!* He'd dated several other girls since then. He had no doubt that Julia had dated other guys as well.

Emerson looked troubled. "An hour ago, I would've agreed with that statement, but I'm no longer so sure." His jaw tightened. "You two kissed last Saturday, as in *really* kissed."

"I know." There lay the problem. Dev lifted his hat again to fist his hand in his hair. "Believe me, I know." He'd not been able to get her or their kiss out of his mind since.

Emerson abruptly straightened, dropping his arms. "Listen, I can handle things here at the store. Why don't you go find her and figure things out? You're not gonna get another moment of peace until you do."

"I can't." Dev's head drooped. "Guess I'm still not ready for that clean break she seems to want so badly."

Emerson sounded stunned. "Wow! You still have it pretty bad for her."

"It is what it is." Dev shrugged and gave his brother a warning look. "This stays between you and me."

Emerson raised two fingers. "Scout's honor."

"You were never a Boy Scout, slick."

"Doesn't mean I'm not honorable."

It was true. Emerson had never betrayed him. With a rigid nod, Dev stomped away to get back to work. Though the day dragged by too slowly, he wasn't near ready for closing time when it rolled around. He wasn't looking forward to being alone with his thoughts throughout the evening and night. He wasn't particularly looking forward to spending time with anyone else, either.

As he climbed into his black Ford pickup, he decided a compromise might be in order. Instead of being alone or suffering through the prying questions of his well-meaning family over dinner, he headed for the horse barn instead.

Emerson's question earlier about whether he missed his rodeo days had hit a little too close to home. Yes, he missed riding broncs and bulls. Yes, he missed the challenge and excitement of pitting his skills against those of other talented riders. As much as he enjoyed co-managing the family store with his twin, what they did for a living wasn't near as exciting as their original plan to make a career on the rodeo circuit.

That's why he'd purchased a new palomino last week — a young quarter horse named Quick Trigger, who was in desperate need of training. The previous owner had sold him because of his unpredictable temperament. However, Dev was convinced that the creature was simply spirited. With a firm hand and the right amount of attention, he had the makings of a decent race horse.

He parked his truck in front of the wide, three-story red barn next to a bright yellow Jeep he'd never seen before. It was probably the latest toy his youngest brother, Fox, had purchased. The guy was always tinkering with one off-roader or another. If Dev had been any less tired, he would've stopped and asked his brother about it, but he really just wanted to work with Quick Trigger for an hour or two. No talking. No people. Just him and his horse.

The wide entrance door of the barn was rolled open. A dry autumn breeze whisked hotly across his cheeks and forehead as he pushed open his truck door and leaped to the ground.

Fox was standing outside the barn, tossing a lime green tennis ball across the nearest pasture fence for his dog, Ghost, to run and fetch. He'd rescued the all-white German Shepherd from a trap in the woods and nursed him back to health. The two of them were nearly inseparable now.

The dog looked more like a wolf than a German Shepherd, which earned him wary looks from Cassidy Farm's many visitors. However, he was as friendly as a lapdog. He took one look at Dev and sprinted joyfully in his direction with the tennis ball. With a woof of happiness, he dropped the slobbery ball on top of the toes of Dev's boots.

"Good boy!" With a chuckle, he reached down to scratch the dog's ears.

In response, Ghost adoringly pushed his head against Dev's hand. Then he snuffled his way up and down the legs of his jeans.

"Traitor," his owner fumed from a few feet away. Fox pushed his dark hair from his eyes and tucked it beneath his Stetson, glaring in mock disapproval at his older brother. "I feed him, train him, and throw his soggy tennis balls, and this is the thanks I get for my trouble. Complete betrayal!"

"Nah, I'm pretty sure his primary interest in me is because I smell like freshly ground beef." Dev smirked at his brother. "I helped package a few racks of it this afternoon at the store."

"And you came here smelling like that?" Fox's heavily tanned features scrunched in doubt. "Way to go, Romeo!"

Dev had no earthly idea why his youngest brother cared what he smelled like or why he was calling him Romeo, for that matter. There was no telling where Fox was concerned, though, since he was known far and wide for his jokes and pranks. At the moment, Dev wasn't in the mood to ask, so he kept walking.

"And crabby, to boot," Fox muttered as his older brother stalked past him.

Dev silently shot out a fist and popped him in the shoulder, making him dance a little to keep his footing.

"Yep! You're all sunshine and roses this evening. I should sell tickets to what's coming next." Fox snorted out a laugh and threw the tennis ball again for Ghost. The dog took off with a yelp of excitement.

Thoroughly fed up with his cryptic comments, Dev stepped inside the barn and made a beeline for his palomino's stall. It was empty. That was strange. He glanced up and down the long aisle. Stalls lined both sides of it, most of them occupied.

"Where are you, Quick Trigger?" He strode slowly down the aisle so he could glance into each stall. He wasn't sure why anyone would've moved his horse, but they'd done so at their own peril. Quick Trigger was neither docile nor obedient. Most folks who got too close to him received a nip on the shoulder or arm.

A quick examination of each stall proved that the horse was no longer in the barn, which Dev found even more puzzling. Because that meant someone had taken his horse outdoors without his permission. The thought of anyone attempting to ride the creature filled him with a healthy mix of apprehension. Quick Trigger wasn't trained well enough to be safely ridden. It was something Dev had been planning to change, starting this evening — just as soon as he located the spirited beast.

Pushing open the rear exit door of the barn, he stopped short at the sight of his horse racing in mad circles. He was working up a lather inside the practice ring.

And he wasn't alone.

Dev's mouth tightened at the sight of Julia Benson standing inside the ring with him. She was positioned in the dead center of it with her back turned to him. One hundred percent of her attention was trained on the tall, caramel-colored creature she was driving in circles with the end of the rope she was twirling. She was waving it at him without touching him with it, all the while urging him to continue running.

She didn't look up even after she pivoted in Dev's direction. Her attention remained solely on the horse, her movements in perfect sync with his.

Dev's gaze narrowed on Quick Trigger, noting the defiant way he was tossing his white mane and the shrill tone to his whinnies. As usual, he was irritated enough to bite, but his anger didn't seem to phase Julia.

She continued running him in circles with sharp commands that grew lower and quieter as the beast grew weary. After his coat grew slick with sweat, she ran him several more laps around the ring. It was as if she was trying to drain the fight straight out of him.

Then she abruptly stopped calling out commands. Pausing in the center of the ring, she waited with her back turned to the horse. The position just so happened to leave her facing Dev.

Their gazes met. His was angry; hers was defiant. He wanted nothing more than to demand why she was interfering with his horse's training. However, he was too afraid of saying or doing anything that would spark the horse into doing her harm. It was more prudent to wait and speak until she was safely on the other side of the fence, out of Quick Trigger's biting and kicking range.

He was forced to watch in stony silence as the horse finally noticed that Julia's rope was dangling motionlessly at her side. He ran a few more strides before stopping. Then he stood against the far perimeter of the fence for a moment, stomping his hooves and twitching his tail.

Dev watched as Julia's slender shoulders grew tense. He braced himself, not knowing what would come next. So help him, if the horse tried to hurt her, he might not have any choice but to put him down. Sick with dread, Dev inched his hand toward the pistol strapped inside the chest holster beneath his shirt.

Julia's gaze followed his movements. Alarm flared in her eyes, making them deepen to an unfathomable shade of blue. She sent him an almost imperceptible head shake.

He ignored her, unbuttoning his shirt and wrapping his fingers around the pistol.

Without warning, Quick Trigger jerked into motion again. He slung his head from side to side and pawed the ground. Then he took a few steps in Julia's direction and stopped.

Dev removed his pistol and took aim, but the horse didn't seem to notice. He took another step toward Julia, and another one. The moment he reached her, he stopped again. Ever so slowly, he lowered his long, regal head and butted her shoulder with it. Oddly enough, he made no attempt to bite her.

Dev felt the wind leave his chest, fully expecting the head butt to be followed by a delayed bite. However, the horse continued to stand there, waiting. Dev's shoulders slumped as he was forced to acknowledge that the impossible had just happened. It was truly a miracle. He wouldn't have believed it if he hadn't seen it with his own eyes, but it was true. The glorious creature had yielded to the woman standing in the center of the ring.

Something like wonder spread across Julia's fine-boned features. "Good boy," she murmured, reaching up to stroke the silky hair above his nose.

Dev hadn't even noticed the lead rope in her hands moving until she expertly looped it around Quick Trigger's neck.

"Good boy," she crooned again, continuing to shower the horse with praise. She reached inside the pocket of her jeans and produced a handful of stubby carrots.

He greedily ate them from her gloved hand before snuffling his way adoringly across her wrist. He continued sniffing his way up her arm and across her shoulder, learning her size, shape, and scent.

"You old reprobate." Dev finally found his voice again. Shoving his pistol back inside its leather sheath, he moved to the fence to rest his elbows on the top slat.

Julia's lush lips twitched as she led the horse in his direction. "Him or me?"

He curled his upper lip at her. "If the shoe fits…"

She reached Dev and handed the lead rope across the fence to him. "Just for the record, your horse is as much of a jerk as you are."

He accepted the lead rope and promptly received

a nip on the edge of his hand. It wasn't as vicious as the last one the horse had given him, but still. With a snort of disgust, he lightly flicked Quick Trigger's mouth and almost got nipped a second time.

"Here." Julia shoved some carrot pieces into his hand.

Dev fed them to the horse before throwing a leg over the fence and climbing inside the ring. He waited until he'd wedged himself between Julia and Quick Trigger before speaking again. "What are you doing here?"

She sniffed. "What does it look like?"

"Interfering." He grated out the word.

"You mean helping," she returned stiffly as she vaulted over the fence to safety. "You're welcome," she added with a mocking little bow.

He couldn't help noticing her wince as she came down on her left foot. His concern escalated all over again as he inwardly considered all the worst-case scenarios. Had Quick Trigger stepped on her? Kicked her? Bit her?

He drew a breath to get a grip. "Did my horse hurt you?" he demanded tightly.

She blinked at him. "You saw what happened."

He glanced pointedly down at her scuffed riding boot. "You're limping."

She shrugged. "I was limping before I got here."

Relief surged through him as he led the horse from the ring back into the barn.

"Why did you come here?" he demanded as Julia fell into step beside him.

"Not to get shot at, that's for sure." She made a face at him.

"I wasn't going to shoot you, and you know it."

"You were seriously going to take out your own horse?" She looked horrified.

"If he hurt you, yes. He's dangerous."

"That's a load of bull." She wrinkled her nose. "He's just misunderstood."

That remained to be seen, though she'd certainly made great progress in proving her point this evening. "Quit dodging the question. Why are you here?"

"You didn't want to talk." She waved a hand. "I did. Still do," she amended with a sigh. "So, I decided to find something besides words to deliver my message."

What message? He fell silent as he tethered Quick Trigger to the grooming station and started to brush him down.

She snatched up a second brush and moved to the other side of the horse. For a few minutes, there was nothing but the sound of bristles sliding against horse flesh.

Dev debated what to say, but he hardly knew where to start. So much time had passed since their last real conversation. So much anger. So much pain. So much regret. And now she was back — kissing him last week, being nice this evening, and messing with his head all over again.

The first accusation more or less slid out of him.

"You can't just come back here and expect us to pick up where we left off."

Julia caught her breath. "Is that what it looks like I'm doing?"

He stopped brushing and leaned across the back of the horse to spear her with a hard look. "Honestly? I have no idea what you're doing. Last week, you said something about wanting to officially break things off with me—"

"Not true." She lifted her chin. "I simply reminded you that we never officially broke up, something I happen to think you owe me before getting engaged to someone else."

He stared at her in astonishment. "What are you talking about?"

She stared back. "You and Rosie McKeever."

Ugh! Just shoot me now. He wasn't sure what rumor Julia had heard. Regardless, he had zero interest in discussing it. Rosie McKeever had made it all too clear in recent months how available she was to any of the Cassidy brothers. None of them returned the sentiment.

He glared at his ex. "Why are you bringing her into this?"

"Are you about to pop the question to her or not?" There was a strange hitch to Julia's voice, like she was either about to start laughing or crying. He wasn't sure which.

He shook his head in disgust. "I can't believe you feel the need to ask that!"

Her long blonde lashes fluttered against her

cheeks. "Just give me the respect of a full break-up before you move on, okay?"

Dev threw his brush down and stomped around the horse to face her. "If you think you can snap your fingers and bring me to my knees again, it's not going to work this time."

She tossed her brush down beside his and faced him, hands on her hips. "I'm just trying to have a conversation with you, Devlin Cassidy." She shook her head in defeat. "And since you refused to talk to me earlier, I tried to do something nice. Hold out the olive branch, so to speak. To show you I'm not the horrible monster you've made me out to be for the past eight years. I'm not." She shook her head again, more vehemently this time.

"I don't think you're a monster." His heart wrenched as the truth spilled out of him. "A spoiled brat, maybe. Someone who's gotten everything she ever wanted, no matter the cost to those around her."

Julia took a stumbling step back, as if he'd slapped her. "Spoiled, huh?"

He shrugged. "It's one of the risks of being an only child, I guess."

"Really?" Her voice grew deceptively calm as her gaze clashed with his and held. "That's rich coming from a guy who's had the entire world handed to him. Two amazing parents who love you to pieces. Five amazing brothers who've always had your back. And a family business on top of everything else. You've never been laid off, never had to job hunt."

He glared at her. "If my life was so perfect, why'd you dump me and run?"

"I didn't. There were just things I wanted more at the age of eighteen than marriage."

"Such as?" He totally got the fact that he'd screwed up and asked her to marry him too soon, but he'd never understood why she'd stayed gone for eight long and lonely years.

"I wanted to see the world, the same as you, Dev. I wanted to make a name for myself, which I did. I wanted something that was mine, I guess. Something no one else could take away from me." Her bosom heaved, and she grew winded as she defended herself.

He stared back angrily. *I could have been yours, and no one could've ever taken me away from you.* But she hadn't seen it that way.

"More than anything," she continued brokenly, "I wanted a mom in my life. My real mom, not some cheap substitute. I always knew it was a stupid, impossible dream; but it never kept me from wanting it."

He frowned at the abrupt turn in their conversation. "I'm sorry you lost your mom." From what he understood, Julia's mom had died when she was a baby. Then her stepmom, whom she'd never gotten along very well with, had died a couple of years ago. It was a double tragedy that no kid should ever have to go through. If Julia was looking for pity points, Dev had plenty to spare in that area. He wasn't sure what it had to do with their current situation, though.

"I was sorry, too. Right up to the point I found out she was still alive."

Wait! What? Dev gawked at her, utterly perplexed. "You mean to tell me your biological mom is…" He didn't know how to finish the sentence.

"Yes. She's alive, Dev. Turns out she left us when I was a baby to pursue a rodeo career. I finally located her a few weeks ago. Or rather, she located me and turned my whole life upside-down. Or maybe she'd finally turned it right-side-up." Julia lifted a hand to her forehead as if she was feeling feverish. "Actually, she's the reason I'm back in town."

"Oh?" His heart sank. As dumb as it was, he'd kind of been hoping he was the reason.

"She insisted I come make things right with Dad before it's too late. Told me the only reason he'd been so hard on me all those years was because he was afraid I'd turn out like her."

"What's that supposed to mean?" Dev wasn't sure what she meant.

"That I'd marry the rodeo like she did, and my career would always come first."

He snorted and glanced away. "She wasn't wrong."

"She wasn't right, either, because I came back."

"For now." He swallowed hard, hating the way her words made old hopes leap painfully back to life.

"For good, Dev. I messed up my leg really bad a

while back. It gets well. Then it goes out again. My rodeo career is over."

He blew out a breath, unsure if he believed her. An injured leg didn't necessarily spell the end of a barrel racing career. The bigger issue, though, was that she hadn't come back to town for him.

He watched her closely. "So, you're not here because you want to be."

"Wrong again." Her expression hardened. "I can afford to live anywhere I want, do anything I want, and be anything I want. I chose to come home."

He threw up his hands. "What do you want from me, Julia?"

"I don't know." She eyed him sadly. "Eight years ago, I wanted you to join me on the rodeo circuit. We had plans together. You backed out."

"My grandfather died. I got pulled into the family business sooner than I planned."

"You never once called or visited me."

"Neither did you." He'd followed her career, though. He had a wall of maps, photographs, and news clippings in his office to prove it. Not that he planned on ever telling her. Instead, he stood toe-to-toe with her, staring her down. If she'd come home to finish destroying him, she was in for a big surprise. Like her, he was harder than he used to be. Tougher. Stronger.

"You're the one who said you wanted to take a break from our relationship," she reminded in a thready voice.

"Not for eight years!" His voice was equally

hoarse. He'd been hurt by her rejection of his marriage proposal. Blind with it. Consumed by it. Still was.

"When we kissed, I felt something." There was no denying the tremble in her voice now. "Like it wasn't over yet between us, but I've made too many mistakes with you to trust my own judgment anymore. So, you tell me. Do you want that clean break we never gave each other, or do you want to try again?"

CHAPTER 3: TALK IS CHEAP

JULIA

Julia's stomach pitched sickeningly while she waited for Dev to respond.

He took his time, forcing her to watch a thousand mercurial emotions cross his strong features.

By the time he started talking again, she'd literally broken into a sweat. "Why? Do you?"

"I asked you first." After taking so long to respond, she couldn't believe he was being so cagey.

His jaw tightened. "The reason I didn't want to talk this morning at the store was because of how long it took you to hunt me down."

She waved a shaky hand in the air. "Dad's been sick. I've been looking after him."

He frowned at that, but didn't pounce on it. "To be honest, I figured you were coming to break up with me, and I was angry you were going to do it in public. Thought you should have the decency to do it in private."

Though her heart leaped with hope at his words, all she did was roll her eyes at him. "It's nice to know you think so little of me."

He shrugged. "What else was I supposed to think?"

"When have I ever deliberately been cruel to you or your family?"

The look he gave her was so full of hurt that she nearly broke down right then and there. Clearly, he'd yet to forgive her for refusing to marry him after high school.

"Listen, Dev, here's the bottom line." She drew a deep breath and took the plunge. "If you want a clean break from me, you're going to have to be the one to do it."

"No." The look he gave her was cold. "You're not making me out to be the bad guy again. Since you were the one to point out that we're still technically dating, you get to be the bad guy and do the dirty work."

A mirthless laugh escaped her. "So, we're still dating, because neither of us wants to take credit for our final breakup?" She hadn't seen this coming.

"Looks like." He shrugged. "Don't worry, though. I can be a much bigger jerk than what you witnessed this evening. Mark my words. The next time we call things off between us, you're going to take off running and never look back." His voice was so low and threatening that she shivered.

"Wow! My boyfriend really hates me." She waved both hands at her flaming face, trying to absorb the fact that they were actually still dating. Heaven knew if Dev didn't want to be with her, he'd have made no bones about breaking things off for good. He was still hurt and angry, but he still cared. Her heart was fluttering so crazily over the discovery that it was making her lightheaded.

"If you don't like it," he snarled.

She burst out laughing again, mainly because she was so close to crying. "You aren't the only one who can be a jerk, Devlin Cassidy. According to a lot of folks in this town, I'm the Queen of Mean. And since I know how mad it's gonna make you, I'll be back at the same time tomorrow." She took a step closer to him, tipping her face sassily up at him. "Interfering in your horse's training all over again."

His gaze dropped to her mouth. Emotion blazed in his icy gaze. "Don't forget I'm packing heat, darling."

She smirked at him. "If you think the only thing I'm packing tonight is carrots, you're sorely mistaken." By now, her left knee was hurting so badly, she figured it was time to make her exit before it reached screaming levels. She started to sweep past him, lost her balance, and nearly toppled into him. To her mortification, she had to grab his arm to steady herself.

To cover her embarrassment, she threatened, "Oh, I'll make your life even more miserable than it already is if you tell anyone my mother is still alive."

"It's not my story to tell," he conceded testily.

"Good, because my dad doesn't know yet, and

I'm not sure how to tell him." The muscles in his forearm flexed warmly beneath her fingers, making her dizzy in response.

"He thinks she's dead, too?"

"Yes. It's a long story. Too long to go into right now. You'll just have to take my word for it." Not wanting his pity, she didn't bother looking up as she dropped her hand from his arm and finished her exodus from the barn.

Fox, who was throwing a ball to his ghostly German Shepherd, threw her a two-fingered salute and yelled goodbye. Unless she was mistaken, he called her Juliette instead of Julia. Then again, she might have misheard. Her entire brain felt scrambled this evening.

She barely made it to her custom Jeep Rubicon before collapsing. She literally had to use one of the roll bars to hold herself up while she yanked open the door and swung herself behind the wheel.

It was a gorgeous vehicle. Just looking at the banana yellow off-roader put her in a better mood. She'd purchased it months ago, though it had only been delivered a few days ago. She'd seriously juiced it up with every option available on the market — convertible top, turbo-charged engine, extra roll bars, and extra spotlights. She'd even installed blue under-carriage lights. Though she'd not told anyone yet, she'd already contacted a realtor to help her purchase a piece of land. If everything went according to her plans, she'd be hosting Chipper's first off-roading races come next spring.

A bum left knee might have cancelled her barrel racing career, but it in no way would keep her from driving tricked out vehicles. Excitement coursed through her veins at the thought, chasing away the worst edge of her pain. It also gave her a much-needed boost of energy, which she used to drive back to her childhood home.

Gosh, but she couldn't wait to build a place of her own and leave her dad's crankiness behind once and for all. Things hadn't gotten any better between them during her eight-year absence. She really wasn't sure why her mother had insisted on her coming home to work on her relationship with him. It felt kind of pointless.

Like most of the other founding families of Chipper, they lived on a ranch. Unlike the Cassidys, who specialized in farming, and the Arlettas, who specialized in raising beef, the Bensons were horse breeders. They were known throughout the west for their prized quarter horses. Because of their reputation, it was pretty easy to track the movement of their horses after they were sold and resold.

That's how she'd found out about Devlin Cassidy's purchase of Quick Trigger. His original buyer had talked her dad into transacting the sale before the horse's training was complete. Instead of continuing the horse's training as promised, he'd then gifted the spirited creature to his spoiled teenage daughter, who'd been heavier on the use of her riding crop than she'd been on kindness. After being bitten a few times, she'd refused to work with him altogether. He'd subsequently languished in their stables for months, growing less predictable and more temperamental by the day.

If Dev hadn't purchased him, the poor horse might've ended up in the slaughter house. What a pity! Because it had taken only one training session with the beautiful palomino to determine that he was, in fact, still trainable. Julia intended to prove it to Dev so long as he'd give her the chance to.

With a delicious shiver at having the perfect excuse to spend more time with him, she turned onto the paved driveway leading to the Silver B Ranch. Pastures stretched on either side of her. As far as the eye could see, quarter horses of all colors were grazing, trotting, and snoozing. They were a stunning sight, like artwork in motion. As long as she lived, she'd never tire of looking at them.

Her cell phone jingled with an incoming call as she drove by the vast white stables where the horses were boarded every night. She mashed the button on her steering wheel to connect the phone wirelessly.

"Hey, hon!" Brooke Flanagan's voice rang cheerfully through the Jeep's cab.

"Hi, Mom." Julia's voice was cautious. "I'm nearly home, so unless you want Dad to hear your voice and know that you're, well..." *Alive.*

"All in good time, sugar." Her biological mother's voice sobered. "Just not tonight, please."

"Do you need something?" Julia drearily eyed her father's two-and-a-half story log home. Thanks to her late stepmother, who'd insisted on a bazillion pricey renovations and expansions, it looked more like a vacation lodge than a home these days. The thought was accompanied by no small amount of guilt for thinking ill of the dead.

"Do I need a reason to call my own daughter?" her mother shot back.

"I don't know how to answer that question." Julia blew out a frustrated breath as she pulled into her father's detached six-car garage. "I guess I'm still getting used to the idea of having a mother."

"Fair enough."

"In case you didn't hear it, I just turned off the motor."

"Okay, I'll make this quick," Brooke Flanagan sighed. "I mainly wanted to see how Cody is doing today. Better, I hope?"

"He's on his third round of antibiotics for the pneumonia, and his blood pressure is stabilizing."

"Thank the Lord," her mother breathed.

Julia sniffed. "Wow! It almost sounded like you care about him or something." Her parents seriously took the prize for having the weirdest dynamics on the planet. Her dad thought her mother was dead. And despite ditching him when Julia was a baby, Brooke Flanagan acted like she was still in love with him.

"Of course I care!"

"Then why doesn't he even know you're alive?"

"Because I, er, sort of faked my death."

"Mom!"

"It's complicated, hon."

"So you keep saying." Julia wanted so desperately to understand.

"Well, we don't have time to get into it now. It was a long time ago. A time in my life when I was really messed up, body and soul. I'm happy to say I'm not that person anymore."

Julia had no idea what to say to that, so she said nothing.

"Just take care of him for me, please," her mother pleaded.

"I'm here, aren't I?"

"Not because you want to be."

"Ain't that the truth! I'm only here because you strong-armed me into it."

"Thank you. You're a good kid."

"I'm twenty-six-years-old," Julia reminded impatiently. "I'm no longer a kid."

"You'll always be my kid." Her mother's voice was infused with affection. Then she changed the subject. "How's Dev? Have you seen him yet?"

"Yes."

"Uh-oh. Does that mean you finally broke things off with him?"

"No."

"You're kidding!"

"It's complicated," Julia grumbled, borrowing one of her mother's favorite words. "Like you said, we don't have time to get into it tonight."

"Just let me get one thing straight before you hang up," her mother pleaded. "Are you still dating Devlin Cassidy?"

"I am, but only because he's insisting that I have to be the bad guy and do the breaking up."

"I see." Her mother sounded amused.

"I don't think you do."

"I see more than you think."

"Just don't get your hopes up about us. We both pretty much made it clear earlier that we're going to do everything we can to get the other person to break up."

"Ouch!"

"You can say that again."

"Ouch!"

They shared a chuckle.

"I'm hanging up now, Mom."

"I love you, sweetheart," her mother said quickly.

"I love you, too, Mom." It was wonderful to finally be able to say those words after all these years.

"How about you prove it by being nice to your dad tonight?"

"For the thousandth time, why do you care?" Julia groaned.

"We both know I'm not going to answer that right now."

With a sound of long-suffering, Julia disconnected the line, knowing she'd stalled long enough. It was time to go make sure her father had taken his last round of medication for the day, even if he took a bite out of her for her efforts. *Ugh!* She briefly dipped her head against the steering wheel, taking a moment to just breathe.

Though she was hoping to shower and soak her

aching leg before her next encounter with her father, she knew she probably wouldn't be that fortunate. She was right.

He met her at the front door, all six feet two inches of evening shadows and bluster. There were bruising circles beneath his eyes as he held the door open for her. "You came back."

She spread her hands in exasperation as she limped past him. "You invited me to stay here, remember? My suitcases are still upstairs."

"Where have you been?" There was more frost at his temples than she remembered, but the same old scowl rode his rugged features. He wore the same old chilly gaze, too. It was as blue as his denim jeans.

"Out," she answered sharply.

"I can see that. What's wrong with your leg?"

"Nothing," she snapped.

He slammed the door behind her. It was loud enough to make her jump. "Why do you bite my head off every time I ask a simple question?"

She shot an angry look over her shoulder as she headed across the two-story entry foyer toward the kitchen. "Because I learned from the best." She tried not to look at the deer heads mounted to the walls and the massive antler chandelier suspended over the front double doors. She'd always hated this part of the house. It was more grisly than homey — another one of her stepmother's many upgrades. Though Julia had made her peace with Tonna Benson before she'd passed, she still thought there were too many traces of the woman left in the house. It was no wonder her father remained so depressed.

He scrubbed a hand through his hair as he followed her, looking suddenly older than his forty-nine years. Instead of zinging another comeback her way, he coughed. And coughed some more. He paused in the arched doorway leading to the kitchen to rest his hand against the wall, still coughing.

As angry as Julia was at him for making the last decade and a half of her life so miserable, she couldn't bear the sound of him struggling to breathe. Blinking back tears, she riffled through the dirty mugs and bowls he'd left scattered across the granite countertop in her absence.

Whirling around to face him, she grated out, "Where's your medicine?"

He blinked at her for a moment, still coughing. Then his icy gaze softened. "Aw, you almost sounded like you cared for a second there."

She straightened, trying to ignore the ache in her leg. "Where are your prescriptions? If you want to get well, you have to take them."

He shrugged. "In the medicine cabinet in the master bathroom."

"Oh, for pity's sake!" she exploded. "Why did you move them?"

His smile was more of a grimace. "Maybe so you wouldn't poison me."

"Haha!" She pivoted around to stomp from the kitchen, but her stomp ended up being more of a hobble.

When she returned to the kitchen, he was brewing coffee. Two cups. It smelled like her favorite chocolate blend. He must have found her hidden stash in the cabinet.

He spoke without turning around. "What's up with your leg? I can tell it's hurting you."

"Tore my ACL." She plopped down on one of the stools at the bar. "Twice."

"Julia!" He whirled around so quickly with the two mugs of coffee that he sloshed one of them over the rim. His hands were shaking when he set them down on the bar in front of her. Instead of sitting, he leaned his palms heavily on the cabinet to fix her with a look she couldn't read. "Is that why your name is no longer on the roster for any rodeos in the region?"

"Wow!" She reached greedily for the nearest mug. "I'm surprised you noticed."

He ignored the jibe. "Which knee?"

"Left."

"Have you had surgery yet?"

"Yep."

"So, you're convalescing? Is that what really brought you into town?" He pulled a wad of paper towels from the iron holder beside the sink, threw them on the tile floor, and used his foot to mop up the spilled coffee.

"No." She scanned the writing on the side of his medicine bottles to make sure she was administering the right dosage. Then she carefully laid out his final round of pills on a napkin. She slid it in his direction.

"Someone found out you were sick and told me." That person had then twisted her arm into returning home to look after him.

"Interesting." He picked up the soiled paper towels and tossed them in the wastebasket by the sink. "Guess that also explains why you're canoodling with a realtor and looking for land."

"Actually, the two issues aren't related." Julia watched her father blandly as he swallowed his pills dry and sipped on coffee afterward. He was one of the toughest guys she'd ever met, even when it came to how he swallowed his pills.

He finally took a seat on one of the stools across from her. "Whatever your reasons, I'm glad you're here."

She nodded and took another slurping sip of her coffee. "You didn't think I'd ever come back."

"No." He ducked his head and stared drearily into his mug. "I'm glad you're here, though. It's been," he glanced around the kitchen, clearing his throat, "awfully quiet around here the last few months."

She reached over to touch his wrist. "Dad, I'm sorry you lost Tonna."

He stared at her hand on his arm. For a moment, she thought he'd shake it off. "Why? You never liked her."

"But you did. I'm truly sorry for your loss." She patted his arm. "For what it's worth, I made my peace with her during her last trip to Dallas to watch me ride."

"She told me." He covered her hand with his, anchoring it more solidly to his arm. "Thanks for doing that."

"No problem."

"Are you here to stay?" His head remained bowed.

"Probably. I still have a few more demons to wrestle, but I'm making some progress."

He snorted. "I take it I'm one of those demons?"

He knew he was, so she didn't bother answering.

"Have you seen Devlin Cassidy yet?"

"Yep."

He glanced up, grinning slightly. "And?"

She shrugged. "And what?" There was no way she was making this easy on him.

"Nothing."

"Your expression says otherwise."

"Fair enough. My expression says I would've paid anything to be a fly on the wall during your confrontation with that Cassidy boy."

"Then you would've found out something nobody else in town knows about us."

His blonde eyebrows shot upward. "I'm listening."

That's a first. "We never broke up, Dad."

She thoroughly enjoyed the look of shock that spread across his features, along with the way his jaw dropped. He tried to say something, coughed, and had to pull his hands away from hers to bury his mouth against his sleeve.

When he finally caught his breath, he wheezed,

"You mean to tell me you two have been dating all this time?"

"Apparently." She took another sip of her coffee. It was cooling off now, making it possible for her to drink it faster.

"I don't get it." He shook his head. "He's been dating other people. Tonna said—" He broke off whatever he was going to say next.

Julia shrugged. "Newsflash, Dad. Tonna wasn't right about everything."

"Don't." He hunched his shoulders over his coffee.

She stood and carried her near-empty mug to the sink. Pouring what was left down the drain, she rinsed out her mug before setting it down. Then she quickly gathered the rest of the dirty dishes off the cabinet and piled them into the same side of the sink.

Glancing over her shoulder at her father, she announced quietly, "I'll wash these in the morning. Goodnight, Dad."

"'Night, baby."

She was floored for a moment by the affection in his voice. It had been a long time since she'd received anything but censure from him.

She hobbled to the long, winding staircase in the entry foyer and let out a gusty sigh as she tipped her head to stare up at it. If anything, the staircase had gotten taller since the last time she'd climbed it. Gripping the banister, she pulled herself painstakingly up the first stair, then the second one.

Fortunately, there was a landing halfway up. She took a few minutes to rest there before continuing on.

Instead of showering when she reached her old bedroom, she turned on the faucets in the garden tub and filled it nearly to the brim. The water was just shy of scalding when she peeled off her jeans and shirt and stepped into it. The heat felt good on her sore leg, more than good. As she scrubbed off the dust and sweat from Cassidy Farm, the sharp pain in her knee subsided to a duller ache.

After toweling off, she applied the herbal wrap that Emerson had sold her earlier. She had no idea if it would do any good, but it certainly couldn't hurt. Then she sank on top of the lilac comforter covering her queen-sized bed and reached for the wide square album resting on her nightstand.

The white leather cover had long since grown dingy with age and handling. Not that Julia had gone to a lot of effort to keep it clean. There was a coffee stain on the upper right-hand corner that she'd never bothered scrubbing off. There were also scratches on the back of the album from the number of times she'd tossed it across the room in anger.

The inside of the wedding scrapbook her stepmother had insisted she put together, however, remained painfully intact. The woman had gifted it to her with the air of someone handing over the Crown jewels. At first, Julia had attempted to refuse the gift, but her father had threatened to take her truck keys away if she didn't comply.

So Julia had done his bidding, as usual. She'd

filled the stupid book with pictures of flowers, dresses, cakes, and venues for her wedding to Devlin Cassidy that had never happened. Long after she'd said no to his marriage proposal, she'd continued to add pictures to the scrapbook — mostly to punish herself for giving him the wrong answer.

She'd finally come to realize that saying no to him was the worst decision of her adult life. It was a regret she'd carry to her grave. She continued to keep the scrapbook as a reminder of how delicate true happiness was. Also, because she couldn't quite bring herself to get rid of it.

She closed it and hugged it to her chest, reflecting about how much of her life was in the book. And not just her mistakes. It contained her hopes and dreams as well. Bits and pieces of her rocky relationship with her stepmother that she'd somehow managed to fix before it was too late. Plus, her journey into womanhood.

Her phone, which she'd dropped on the comforter, buzzed with an incoming text message. She reached for it and grew still at the name of the sender. It was from Fox Cassidy.

She clicked open the message, which turned out to be a single photo with no words. He must have snapped it before Dev had arrived. It was a picture of her and Quick Trigger working together in the training ring. Fox had managed to capture both the horse's majesty and her own determination. Both Quick Trigger's mane and her blonde ponytail were flying in the wind. There was so much wild beauty and raw emotion in the picture that it made a lump form in her throat.

As she hugged the scrapbook tighter, she knew she would add another picture to it tomorrow, the first one in months. Though the wedding in the scrapbook had never taken place, it seemed that her and Dev's story was destined to continue on, anyway.

I'm dating Dev Cassidy!

The tears Julia had been holding in all evening finally broke loose. Instead of giving her a headache like they normally did, she felt relieved. Her confrontation with her high school sweetheart had been a long time coming. Not once, though, had she imagined it would end up like this.

With us still together.

She was surprised her dad had taken it as well as he had. Dev's family, on the other hand, was probably going to pitch a fit when they found out. She could hardly blame them.

CHAPTER 4: SHOCKING REVELATIONS

JULIA

Julia slept in the next morning and decided to take it easy the rest of the day. It was the only way she had a shot at being in good enough shape to continue Quick Trigger's training.

Her realtor met her at the crack of noon in front of the next piece of real estate she was recommending that they tour. She pulled her beige sedan crossways with Julia's Jeep, motioning for her to roll down her window.

Julia complied. "Hey, Dixie! Thanks for setting this up."

The realtor tossed back her shoulder-length salt and pepper hair, smiling. "My pleasure. It's not often I get to show land to a kid whose diaper I changed twenty-six years ago."

Julia caught her breath. "You knew my mom?"

"Still do, kiddo." Though guarded, sympathy wafted across her expression.

"Of course, you do," Julia whispered as the

details clicked into place. Brooke Flanagan was the person who'd emailed Julia her first real estate listing. It was clear now that her mother had deliberately sent her to a trusted friend.

Dixie spread her hands wryly. "If you have questions, all you have to do is ask."

"Okay." Julia briefly closed her eyes. "Here's the first one." She opened her eyes. "What are the odds of us touring this property from inside my Jeep?"

Dixie chuckled. "I call shotgun!" She pulled forward to park on the shoulder. Then she stepped out of her car with a folder in one hand and a silver coffee thermos in the other. She held the folder between her teeth while she opened the passenger door of the Jeep and climbed inside.

Then she removed the folder from her mouth to balance it on her knees. "Nice wheels." Her sharp gaze roved over the black leather seats and chrome accessories.

"Thanks. It's like having a second man in my life." Julia shot her a sly look from beneath her lashes, dying of curiosity to know how much the woman already knew about her.

"So, I've heard. You and Dev Cassidy, eh?" Dixie smoothed a hand down her white blouse before clicking her seatbelt in place.

"Word travels fast," Julia murmured, hitting the gas and rolling forward into the gravel driveway.

"That's how small towns work." When they came to a halt beside the entrance keypad, Dixie handed her a sticky note with a four-digit number written on it. "Punch in the number and hit the pound sign," she instructed.

Julia did so, and the black iron gate in front of them rolled open. She handed back the sticky note. "Does the security gate remain with the property?"

"It does." Dixie pointed out the property's highlights as Julia continued driving down the gravel road. "There's a four-stall metal garage ahead. The owner has been storing his tractor and mower deck there. Said to make him a reasonable offer if you want him to leave it behind."

"Why's he selling so much acreage?" Julia was surprised to discover over a hundred acres was for sale just down the road from her father's ranch. It was strange he hadn't already snapped it up to add to his estate.

Dixie set her coffee thermos in one of the cup holders on the console to free up her hands. Then she ticked off the reasons on her fingers. "Number one, this land technically isn't on the market." She paused a beat. "Yet."

Julia frowned. "Then why—"

"He owes your mom a favor. That's why."

"You mean I don't have any competition for this purchase?" Julia gulped, wondering how this latest bit of information would affect her chances at negotiating a good price.

"That's exactly what I mean. If you don't buy it, he's going to keep it."

"Oh, sheesh! I'm not sure this is something I want to get involved in." Julia feathered her brakes, debating whether to turn around and leave. "What kind of favor are we talking about?"

"The family kind. Pete Flanagan is your mom's brother. She bailed him out of a few sticky financial situations during his bull riding days."

"I have an uncle?" Julia gazed at her realtor in amazement.

Dixie shrugged and reached for her coffee thermos again. "Like I said, you're welcome to ask me anything you want."

Julia brought her Jeep to a halt and pressed her hands to her pounding chest. "I don't even know where to start."

"How about at the beginning?"

"Where's the beginning?" Julia cried piteously, feeling lost.

"Your parents met on the rodeo circuit. Neither of them were in church at the time. You came along before they were ready to become parents. He did the honorable thing and proposed, but she refused."

Julia's stomach quivered with sickness. "Are you saying my parents never married?"

"He proposed several times. She kept saying no."

"Why?" Just when Julia was starting to get her feet under her, it felt like her whole world coming unraveled again.

Dixie raised and lowered her shoulders help-lessly. "I've asked myself that question at least a hundred times, and the only answer I can come up with is this. She didn't think she was good enough for him. Probably thought she was doing him a favor.

She was raised in foster care. Never went to college. Battled a drinking problem for years. In contrast, your daddy was from a big ranching family. Wealthy. Successful. Became one of the founding families of this town when Chipper finally incorporated."

Julia gripped the steering wheel. "I'm sorry, but that's no reason to leave a baby behind. Or the man she—" She abruptly paused to give the woman beside her a pained looked. "Did she even love him?"

"Of course, she did, Julia! Your mother is the most loving person I've ever met. She'd give the shirt off her back to anyone she cares for. And her skin. I think that's how they got through to her." Her mouth tightened angrily.

"They?" Julia shook her head. "I'm not following you."

Dixie drew a heavy breath. "I'm sorry. I probably shouldn't have said that."

"Don't you dare stop there!"

"If you insist," her realtor sighed. "I've always suspected someone paid her to leave town. I can't prove it, though, and she refuses to talk about it."

"Who would do such a thing?" The moment the question left her lips, Julia knew the most likely answer. She'd never been close with her paternal grandparents for one simple reason. As the well-to-do owners of a tractor supply store in Dallas, they'd always refused to have anything to do with her and her father — right up until they perished in a tragic yachting accident. Julia had grown up assuming they must have had some sort of falling out with their only son, but maybe it was more than that.

"It's not my story to tell, dear." Dixie's voice was gentle.

"I think I already know it," Julia supplied bitterly. "I suspect my father disappointed his snobby parents by falling in love with the wrong woman, and they didn't want anything to do with the child that resulted from their relationship."

"Again, only your mother can fill in the details for you." Dixie sipped on her coffee and lapsed into silence.

Julia mulled over everything she'd learned, growing angrier by the second. "It still doesn't explain why my mother would take money from them," she stormed.

Dixie studied her sorrowfully over the top of her insulated thermos. "Remember the financial difficulties I told you about, dear?"

"Uh-huh."

"Her brother had gotten into some trouble with the law. She needed the money to bail him out of jail."

"Oh." The air seeped out of Julia. "You think she took the money to help him?"

"I know it beyond a shadow of a doubt, dear. I have no idea why she faked her death on the way out of town."

"Oh, my lands, Dixie! What happened after that?"

Dixie shrugged. "She returned to the rodeo circuit and made a big name for herself."

"How big?" It was so much to absorb that Julia felt like she was choking on it.

"Ever heard of the Silver Streak?"

Julia's lips parted on a gasp. "Everybody in the rodeo business has heard of her!" The Silver Streak was a woman only seen in public with the upper half of her face painted like a masquerade mask. Rumor had it she wore the theatrical colors to cover a hideous set of scars. Folks had speculated on everything from birth defects to burn scars. Regardless, the woman held world records in barrel racing, team roping, and breakaway roping. She'd been inducted into the Rodeo Hall of Fame and was reputed to be the richest woman in rodeo history.

Julia hadn't recognized her without the paint. Not when they met at church for the first time on her twenty-sixth birthday, and not when they visited a restaurant together afterward. She hadn't seen her mother in person since — only that one time.

She had to take several deep breaths to get her heart rate back under control. "I want to buy this property," she blurted. It felt like a piece of it already belonged to her, since she'd apparently been part of its price years ago. "How much is my uncle asking for it?"

"He said if you decided to move forward with the purchase, to tell you it's his gift to you."

A gift? Julia gripped her steering wheel tighter. "Correct me if I'm wrong, but did you not just finish telling me the price of the tractor and mowing deck was negotiable?"

"I did. I honestly think it was Pete Flanagan's way of saying he wants to meet you."

Julia's breath whooshed out of her. "So, they're mine to keep if I agree to…" She stopped and swallowed hard.

"Yes. He said he'll bring you the keys the day he signs the deed over to you."

"Sold to the girl in the yellow Jeep!" Julia started laughing. It was either that or start crying.

"Congratulations!" Dixie reached over to squeeze her shoulder. "Welcome home, kid."

Julia's laughter morphed into a few happy tears. "Clearly, my mother and I have a lot to discuss." She couldn't believe how much the woman had kept from her. It was truly astonishing. "She's been so secretive up to this point." *And now I know why. She faked her death, for pity's sake!*

Dixie nodded ruefully. "She didn't want to overwhelm you by saying too much too soon. Sometimes it's better to absorb things in slow degrees."

"Huh!" Julia's eyes widened. "My uncle just gave me over a hundred acres. Nothing slow about that."

"One-hundred and twenty-four acres to be exact, dear." Dixie's hazel eyes glistened with unshed tears.

Another thought struck Julia, making her quick to assure the woman. "I'll make sure you get a commission out of this." It was the least she could do for someone who'd spent so many hours researching property and showing her around town.

"Already taken care of," Dixie assured softly.

"No way. Huh-uh." Julia shook her head vehemently. "You're not doing this for free. My family's drama is not your problem."

"I couldn't disagree more." Dixie produced a business card and held it out to Julia. "Most people assume the title of my real estate business is my last name, but it's not. My real name is written on the back."

Puzzled, Julie accepted the card and flipped it over to scan what was written there. Then she burst into another peal of laughter. "Dixie Flanagan, huh? I should've known. I guess this makes you my aunt?"

"It does, indeed, dear. Your aunt by marriage." Dixie held out a hand as if they were meeting for the first time. "I'm Pete's wife."

Ignoring her hand, Julia unclasped her seatbelt so she could lean across the console and envelop the woman in a hug.

Dixie squeezed her shoulders before letting her go. "Both Pete and your mama will be driving into town later this week. It'll create quite a stir, of course." She smiled tightly. "The last time Pete was in town, he was arrested. The last time your mother was here, she was, well…alive."

"The gossip mill is going to have a heyday with this." Julia leaned back against the seat cushion, trying to imagine what her father's reaction to the news would be.

Dixie sniffed. "Like you, your mama is a world-renowned barrel racer. I doubt the opinions of a few small-minded people will make her so much as blink these days."

————

Dev was heavily distracted on the job all morning. Right after lunch, he knocked over a trio of candles from a shelf, shattering them loudly and sending glass shards to Kingdom Come.

Emerson jogged his way with a broom and dustpan, holding them out with a note of glee shining in his gaze.

"Don't say it," Dev growled, accepting the broom and dustpan.

Emerson mimed zipping his mouth closed and backed away with his hands raised in self defense. He was laughing uproariously, though, his shoulders shaking and his mouth stretched open in a howl of silent mirth.

Dev shook his fist at him and went to work cleaning up the mess. Before closing time, he'd additionally tripped over a garden gnome and smashed his thumb inside the cash drawer.

"Bro," Emerson muttered as he bagged their last customer's purchases. "You're supposed to remove your hand *before* shutting the drawer."

Dev longed to wipe the smirk off his twin's face with his fist, but he refrained.

After Emerson locked the front doors for the day, he turned around to the counter, where Dev was counting the cash drawer, and exploded, "What on Earth has gotten into you?"

Dev kept counting. "Let it go, Emerson."

"Over my dead body!"

"Dead is exactly what you're going to be if you don't let it go," Dev growled. He threw the handful of coins he was counting back in the drawer, since he'd long since lost count of them. "In case you didn't notice, I'm trying to count money here."

"I'll do it," his twin offered, joining him behind the counter.

"Fine." Dev relinquished the drawer to him and reached beneath the cabinet to grab the item he'd purchased earlier. "Any chance you're willing to close up as well?"

"Sure, but you owe me."

"Add it to my tab." Dev stalked to the bakery on the far side of the store to fill a pastry bag with some of the leftover kolaches and danishes. He and his brothers took turns polishing off the bakery goods each day, and it had been a while since he'd last done so.

"Looks like you're eating for two tonight," Emerson noted casually.

"If you're inviting yourself along, the answer is no." Dev headed for the rear exit, since he'd parked behind the building.

"At least tell me where you're headed," Emerson wheedled.

"To the barn. I've got a date with Quick Trigger." *And my girlfriend, who's refusing to break up with me.* He was looking forward to their coming encounter way more than he should have.

"If you say so, Romeo." Emerson's voice was sly.

Dev gave him a dark look, but kept walking. It

sounded like his twin had been talking to Fox. No surprise there. Fox couldn't keep a secret to save his life.

Dev leaped inside his truck, revved the motor, and nearly clipped the edge of the store sign on his way out of the parking lot. *Shoot!* At the rate he was going, he was probably going to die during tonight's training session with Quick Trigger.

Somehow, he made it to the horse barn on the other side of the ranch without any more mishaps. His heart pounded — first with excitement, then with dread — to note that Julia's yellow Jeep was already parked along the side of the building. She was nowhere in sight. He hoped that didn't mean she was back in the blasted horse ring alone with his demon of a horse.

He yanked open his truck door so fast that he almost dropped the bakery bag. *Pull it together, Cassidy!* He couldn't remember the last time he'd felt like he had two left feet and ten left thumbs. Wait. Yeah, he could. It was the last time Julia had been in town.

She hadn't been too popular back in high school. Their graduating class of thirty-five students, which had been overwhelmingly female, had labeled her a rich snob. One classmate had gone as far as to say that Julia's most redeeming quality had been the fact that she'd been dating a Cassidy brother.

He'd wholeheartedly disagreed. She'd been runway beautiful and ridiculously talented even back then. She'd also been married to the rodeo back then. He could see that now. It was inevitable that someone as gifted as her would spread her wings and fly from their small town. He should've never tried to stop her. Proposing to her at the age of eighteen had been jumping the gun. He should've waited.

Fox was outside the barn, throwing tennis balls again.

Dev grimaced at him. "If you think you're being subtle—"

"I'm not," Fox interrupted cheerfully, jabbing his thumb at the barn. "If you're looking for your girl, she's in the training ring."

Dev's jaw tightened. "I was worried she might be." He stomped past his brother and made a beeline down the hallway between the horse stalls. Pushing open the back door, he halted in amazement.

Julia was standing in the center of the ring again, swinging her rope. Quick Trigger was running circles around the ring like the evening before. As she slowly pivoted in Dev's direction, he noted that she was still favoring her left leg. He also noticed that she winced a little each time she put her weight down on it. She hadn't been joking about her injury.

He moved closer to the fence to rest a boot on the lower slat, watching her intently. As unhappy as he was about the risks she was taking with his unpredictable horse, he had to admit she seemed to know what she was doing.

She repeated the same training sequence from the evening before, running Quick Trigger until he was tired. Then she turned her back on him and waited for the animal to come to her.

Which he did again, the traitor!

Dev's chest swelled with pride at the sight of the tall beast nudging his girlfriend's shoulder like a besotted kitten. Yep, she most definitely knew what she was doing, which didn't make him want to wring her neck any less for the risks she was taking.

He watched as she produced a bag of carrots and apple slices to spoil his palomino with. "He likes you," he admitted once it was safe to talk again.

"I like him, too." Julia led the creature to where Dev was leaning on the fence. "In case you're wondering, I have a much better track record with horses than people."

Dev accepted Quick Trigger's lead rope. The horse tried to nip his hand, but Julia stuffed another few slices of apple into his mouth, distracting him from his antics.

It was such a kind, unselfish, and wholly unconscious gesture that it had to mean she still cared for him. He leaned across the fence to tip her face up to his, seeking answers. What he read in her gaze made him lean in to fuse his mouth to hers.

She broke off the kiss way too soon to climb over the fence and join him outside the ring.

He dropped the lead rope, allowing Quick Trigger to freely roam around the practice ring. Then he leaned back against the fence railing and reached for her again.

"What are you doing, Dev?" Julia didn't offer any resistance as he took her in his arms.

"What does it look like?"

"I know you're about to kiss me, but why?" she demanded. "You've made it clear you don't even like me."

That wasn't true, but he didn't feel like arguing. "If you've got any objections, you can always break up with me."

Her gaze narrowed on his. "You wish!"

Not even a little, darling. He was ravenous to feel her mouth beneath his again. If she didn't hurry up and kiss him, he might lose his mind.

Without breaking eye contact, she stood on her tiptoes to wrap her arms around his neck. "I'm a very patient woman, Dev Cassidy. Mark my words. You *will* be the one to do any breaking up that's gonna happen."

The only thing he could feel breaking at the moment was his willpower to resist her. With a groan of impatience, he palmed the back of her neck and brought his mouth down on hers.

She gasped and kissed him back, clinging to him like a lifeline.

His frustrations from the day vanished beneath her touch. For a moment, they were two high schoolers again, glorying in the magic of their first kiss. "Jules," he rasped, raising his mouth enough to get the words out. "If you don't want this, tell me to stop."

"Don't stop," she whispered. When she touched

her mouth to his again, he was lost. Or found. He wasn't sure which. All he knew was that he was still in love with her. *Correction.* He'd never stopped loving her, and he was never going to.

He kissed her even after he felt the dampness of tears on her cheeks. Come to think of it, his face felt damp, too. He kissed her until the ache in his chest became bearable again. When he finally let her up for air, he rested his forehead against hers.

"I'm never going to end things between us. You know that, right?"

"I'm glad," she whispered. "It would break me if you did."

Her words sank into the deepest, loneliest part of his soul like a healing balm. "It would finish breaking me, too," he confessed raggedly.

"So, where does this leave us, Dev?" Her voice was shaky.

"Dating." A chuckle rumbled from deep within his chest. "Definitely dating."

"I doubt either of our families is going to be thrilled about us getting back together."

"Don't care." He pressed his cheek to hers, mingling their tears.

"Yes, you do," she scolded softly.

"Fine. I care. It doesn't change how I feel about you, though."

She pulled back suddenly to gaze up at him. "How *do* you feel about me?"

He traced the line of her cheek and chin with his thumb. "Like the Lord is giving me another chance to love you the way you deserve to be loved, and I don't want to screw it up." He drank in her glistening blue eyes and the light of wonder spreading across her features.

"Dev, that is seriously the most wonderful thing anyone has ever said to me." Her lush lips bowed upward. "Even so, I wouldn't mind having you to myself for a few days. Having this to ourselves." She snuggled closer.

A ribbon of fear threaded its way through his chest. "You mean you don't want to tell anyone about us getting back together?"

She rolled her eyes at him. "It's not like we're being dishonest or anything since we never officially broke up."

Though he didn't want to scare her off again, he didn't think now was the time for dishonesty. "Suit yourself, but I wouldn't mind telling the whole world you're mine."

She shuddered, but made no move to leave his embrace. "Maybe I'm just being a coward."

He gazed at her with concern. "Okay, I'll bite. What are you afraid of?"

"I'm not as strong as you think, Dev," she sighed.

"Welcome to the club, darling!" He cradled her face between his hands. "Please assure me you're here to stay."

She caught her lower lip between her teeth. "I bought a hundred and twenty-four acres of land in town today."

"A hundred and—"

She made a rueful sound. "Technically, my uncle gifted it to me. An uncle I didn't even know I had."

He snorted out a laugh. "Dare I ask what you're planning on doing with all that land?"

She stared back defiantly. "I'd like to build a racetrack."

He raised his eyebrows at her. "What sort of race-track?" Surely, she didn't plan on going head to head with the rodeo grounds downtown.

"Off-roading vehicles. Monster trucks. Maybe even dirt bikes." She tilted her head challengingly at him. "Between the rodeo grounds and my racetrack, we could turn Chipper into a sporting paradise. We might need a few more hotels to hold all the tourists, though." She shifted from one foot to the other, warming to the subject, and winced when her weight settled on her injured leg.

"That's it. Inside you go, cowgirl." Dev pushed away from the fence, bending to hook an arm beneath her knees. As he lifted her in his arms, she gave a small gasp of pain and shifted restlessly in his grasp.

"What about Quick Trigger?" she protested.

"He'll be fine for a few minutes. I brought something with me that should help your leg."

"Who said there was anything wrong with my leg?"

At his hard look, she relented. "Fine. I tore my ACL. I'm still recovering from the last surgery."

He bared his teeth at her. "You have no business being out there in the training ring like that."

"It was the only way to get your attention," she reminded irritably. "You refused to talk to me, and—"

He twirled her inside the nearest empty horse stall and caught her mouth in another slow and tender kiss. When he raised his head, she gave a breathless chuckle. "You were never all that big on talking, were you?"

He kissed her again as he set her gently down on a bench against the wall. Then he jogged back into the aisle to fetch the two bags he'd brought with him. Between delicious bites of kolaches and danishes, he rolled her jeans above her knee to apply the herbal wrap.

"Since when do you have an uncle in town?" He sought to distract her while he tended to her healing knee.

"Believe me, it's news to me, too." Her smile held a note of incredulity. "Turns out my realtor, Dixie, is married to him, which is probably why my mom sent me her realtor listing." Julia's story spilled out about how her parents had met and fallen in love, but never married. Her words slowed as she tried to describe her uncle's trouble with the law and the drastic measures her mother had taken to protect him.

"If everything my aunt says is true, they've turned their lives around since then. Both of them. He's been a law-abiding citizen for over twenty-five years, and she finally got some help for her alcohol addiction and started going to church. Oh, and they're coming into town to visit me later this week. I, er, hope that's not going to be a problem for us." She waved awkwardly between them.

"Why would it?" He was both taken aback by the question and relieved, quite frankly, that it explained her current reluctance to go public with their relationship.

"People are going to talk." She wrinkled her nose at him. "I hope it doesn't have too negative of an effect on Cassidy Farm."

"We'll weather whatever we have to weather," he assured her firmly.

"Dev…" She sounded uncertain.

He looked undeterred. "I'd like to suggest a compromise to prove that we're in this together."

"What is it?" The look she gave him was so cautiously hopeful that it squeezed his heart.

"Let's tell our families we're dating. Just our families and no one else. And whenever it finally gets out to others, it gets out."

"Okay." She gave him a tremulous smile. "If you truly think this is the best way to handle things."

"I do." They were two words he'd waited a long time to say to her. He hoped to say them again soon in a different capacity. One that involved giving Julia the ring he'd held on to for the past eight years.

This time, though, he wasn't going to rush things between them. He was going to wait until he was sure her answer was the one he wanted to hear.

CHAPTER 5: CONFESSIONS
DEVLIN

Dev and Julia returned to the riding ring to work with Quick Trigger a little longer. They stayed outside until the sun set and the stars began to pop out. He took the final turn inside the ring, allowing her to coach him through one of her unique training methods.

Then they led Quick Trigger back into the barn to brush him down. Dev scrounged up a stool and made Julia sit on it while they worked.

"Bossy!" She took a seat on it, wrinkling her nose at him.

"You love me anyway," he taunted, stooping down to plant another lingering kiss on her.

"I do," she confessed against his lips. "So much. I never stopped."

Her words made him deepen the kiss. He only stopped when he heard the sound of clapping from behind him. Dragging in a bracing breath of air, he turned around, fully expecting to face Fox.

Instead, he found himself facing three of his brothers instead of one — Fox, Emerson, and Asher.

"Well?" A grin stretched from the unblemished side of Asher's face to the side riddled with burn scars. He'd been permanently marked by a freak fire a few years back. "You two got something to tell the family?" He adjusted his Stetson to take a closer look at them. Though he served as the ranch manager at Cassidy Farm, it didn't stop him from getting his hands dirty in the barn. Straw was sticking to the hem of his jeans, which probably meant he'd been helping feed the cows.

"Yeah." Dev squared his shoulders. "The thing is, Julia and I never officially broke up. We had a disagreement and took a break from our relationship. It lasted longer than either of us intended — long enough for both of us to assume things were over between us. But they aren't." He twisted his head to catch her gaze. "It's not ever going to be over between us."

Fox gave a joyful whoop and threw his hat in the air. He had to take a few jogging steps backward to catch it. The barn erupted into chuckles.

Asher stepped forward with his arms outstretched. "I'm happy for you."

Dev moved into his oldest brother's embrace to slap him on the back. "Thanks." He lowered his voice so only Asher could hear. "Just so you know, she's a little worried about what our families will think about us getting back together."

"I've got this." Asher's voice was matter-of-fact.

He strode up to Julia. She tried to stand at his approach, but he rested his hands on her shoulders to keep her seated on the stool. "Dev loves you, which means we all love you. That's how it works with us Cassidys."

Her eyes glistened with wonder as she caught Dev's gaze. "Asher, that's really sweet of—"

He swooped down to kiss her cheek, buying her amazed silence. "Welcome back to town. If you ever try to leave again, there are six Cassidy brothers who just might drag you back by your toenails. Figured you deserved a warning."

"Thanks." Her laughter held a damp note that made Dev want to hug his oldest brother again for his kindness to her. "I'll keep that in mind."

"She's the new owner of a hundred and twenty-four acres here in Chipper," Dev bragged to no one in particular. Though he hadn't expressly asked her permission, he hoped she didn't mind him disclosing that fact.

"Whoa!" Fox swaggered her way to plant a kiss on the opposite cheek as Asher had. "What're you planning on doing with that much land?"

"Believe it or not, I'm going to build a racetrack," she announced, glancing excitedly around their huddle.

Fox gave another whoop that was louder than the first. He brandished both hands dramatically in her direction. "Y'all, meet my new best friend!"

She chuckled, still looking a little worried about

how the brothers would receive the rest of what she had to say.

Dev wanted to reassure her, but some things she was simply going to have to figure out for herself.

"Not that we aren't thrilled about the idea of a racetrack," Emerson's gaze shone with genuine interest and approval as he finally broke into the conversation, "but why the career change?" He glanced down at the herbal wrap around Julia's knee.

She caught her lower lip between her teeth. "It's not yet common knowledge, but I recently suffered a career-ending injury. I was pretty discouraged about it until my mom suggested returning home and—"

"Your mom? Wait a sec!" Emerson's blonde head spun between Dev and Julia. "I thought—"

"So did I," Julia assured him gently. "It's a long story that I'm still trying to wrap my brain around." She shot Dev an apologetic look. "I'm sorry, babe. I know we agreed to keep things quiet for a few days, but your family deserves to know the truth."

Thank you, Lord! He sent up a silent prayer of gratitude that she felt the same way as he did about the situation.

"My dad doesn't know my mom is alive," she disclosed quietly. "For reasons I don't understand, and may never understand, she faked her death when I was a baby and left town. Then she made it big on the rodeo circuit."

"How big?" Fox's dark gaze flashed with fascination.

She caught Dev's gaze and waited for him to nod

before taking the plunge. "Have you ever heard of the Silver Streak?"

For an answer, Fox took a knee in front of her. "Permission to stand in the presence of such greatness, my lady."

"Oh, please!" she scoffed.

"I mean it," he pleaded mockingly.

Dev shot his twin a warning look. The last thing he needed was for any or all of the Cassidy men to scare his girlfriend off tonight.

"I'm not worthy to—" To Dev's relief, Fox's antics were cut blessedly short by Asher and Emerson lifting him bodily to his feet.

"My apologies for our youngest brother's exuberance." Asher gave her a long-suffering look. "Since you don't have any siblings, it would be hard to explain the difficulties of keeping a younger one in line. Suffice to say it's the biggest trial of my adult life."

Emerson nodded. "And the bane of our existence."

"More like the pain of our existence," Dev cut in, chuckling. He was relieved to see that she looked more entertained than alarmed.

"Aw!" Unless he was mistaken, Julia was actually starting to feel sorry for his youngest sibling. She shot Fox a sympathetic smile. "Is he really that bad?"

"Yes," the other brothers chorused so loudly that she burst out laughing.

"Alright, then." She shrugged apologetically at Fox.

"What can I say?" Fox sent her a hopeless shrug. "The persecutions that accompany being the youngest of six brothers are endless."

Dev affectionately slapped Fox's Stetson over his eyes. "Stop fishing for pity points from my woman. It was a democratic process, and you were out-voted." As his brothers noisily filed out of the barn at long last, he strode back to Julia and held out his hands.

She curled her fingers around his and used their joined hands to pull herself to her feet. "Thank you," she said simply.

"For what?" He couldn't resist cuddling her close again. It was so good to have her back in his life and in his arms. He was so grateful. So happy. So complete again.

"For allowing me to be a part of all of this." She gazed dreamily around the barn.

"Surely, you're not referring to my annoying brothers," he teased.

"Oh, but I am! Family is such a beautiful thing," she sighed. "There's nothing more wonderful." Her voice grew softer. "Nothing I've ever wanted more."

His eyebrows stretched upward. Her expression was so wistful that he had to ask. "Nothing?" He knew it was a painful topic for them both, but he'd assumed her career meant more to her than anything else.

"Nothing." She shook her head. "Not my championship titles, not the buckles that came with it, or even the money. There was a time when I thought I wanted those things. Only after I got them did I realize how wrong I was. I, er..." She dropped her gaze as if no longer able to bear meeting his. "I've asked myself thousands of times what my life would've been like if I'd given you a different answer to your question eight years ago." When she next raised her gaze to his, she looked so shamefaced that it took his breath away. "There's nothing I wouldn't do to take back the way I hurt you, Dev. Absolutely nothing!"

He was moved beyond words by her confession. She wasn't just telling him that she still loved him. She was telling him that she wished she'd married him. That she regretted every year, month, and day they'd spent apart as much as he did.

"When I came back to town," she continued in a trembly voice, "I was hoping — no, I was praying — that I would get the chance to tell you that someday."

All he could do was pull her closer to press his cheek against hers. Words alone didn't feel like an adequate response to what she'd shared with him. However, he could sense she was waiting for him to say something.

He could only think of one thing to say. "Would you ride with me to my office, Jules?"

"Tonight?" She looked surprised.

"Yes. Tonight." He tenderly touched her cheek, gazing deeply into her eyes. "There's something I need to show you there." He hadn't originally planned on showing it to her at all, but he suddenly felt that he should.

"Okay," she said. "I'll just—" The rest of what she

was about to say ended in a squeal as he hooked an arm beneath her legs like he'd done earlier and lifted her into his arms.

He carried her to his truck, not caring how many brothers or ranch hands witnessed them together. He hadn't been kidding when he'd declared he was ready to tell the world about their relationship. He'd waited eight years for this moment. He had no interest in waiting another day longer.

Instead of depositing her on the passenger side of the truck, he set her on the driver's side and shimmied in beside her.

Giggling, she scooted over a few inches. Very few inches. She was all but sitting in his lap when he started the motor.

He leaned in for another long, slow kiss before releasing the parking brake and driving in the direction of his family's store.

"I've missed you," she murmured as the pastures rolled past them on both sides of the road. "I've missed us. This." She fluttered a hand at the window.

"Me, too." He knew she wasn't referring to the cattle grazing on the other side of the glass. Or the sinking rays of sunset. Or the deepening shadows of dusk. She was referring to the blessings of family and home. Of love and togetherness.

The moon was rising like a fat white ball over the red barn that housed the Cassidy Farm store. He drove around to the back entrance and parked in front of the door.

"Wow!" Julia pointed at the sky. "The moon is so big and bright that it almost looks fake."

"It does," he agreed. A wolf howled in the distance as they exited the truck. To Dev, it felt like an eerie reminder of how fragile and precious love was. It strengthened his determination to protect it at all costs in the coming days.

A night breeze whistled across the otherwise empty parking lot as he dug his key to the store from his jeans and unlocked the back door to let them inside. He flipped on a light switch, flooding the administrative area with light. Emerson's office was to the left. Dev's was to the right.

He tugged Julia toward it and pushed open the door.

She gazed around the room. "This is nice!" There was a tinge of awe in her voice. "Really nice! I'm going to go out on a limb here and say you had a little help decorating it."

"Naturally." He had no trouble giving credit where credit was due. "If it involves decorating any corner of Cassidy Farm, you can rest assured my mother had a hand in it." Fortunately, Claire Cassidy had excellent taste. He followed Julia's gaze, attempting to see the place through her eyes.

His mother was a big fan of country decor, but she also possessed a classy streak a mile wide. She additionally had a knack for tucking state-of-the-art technology throughout their ranch. The result was an antique executive desk anchored on a Persian rug in the center of his office. It was her favorite shade of cherry wood. A matching cabinet with drawers served as his filing cabinet. His TV and printer were tucked behind the doors of a massive display cabinet against the wall. He kept the doors propped open during business hours and shut them before he left for the day.

What he'd brought Julia to see tonight, however, was hidden behind the screen he'd left pulled down. His desk faced the screen. So did the overhead projector. A modest-sized conference table with four chairs rested in front of it.

Dev moved behind his desk to open the center drawer and withdraw a remote control. Pointing it at the screen, he mashed the button to retract it. The screen slowly rolled upward, revealing the magnetic dry erase board behind it. He'd affixed countless newspaper clippings to it, photographs, and printouts of online news articles.

All of them were about Julia. They highlighted her biggest accomplishments during the eight years she'd been gone from Chipper — her awards, records, and winnings. There were photographs of her barrel racing, team roping, and breakaway roping. There were photographs of her holding up trophies and accepting belt buckles. There was even a special write-up about how she'd held the world record for three years straight in barrel racing.

Julia limped closer to the board, reaching out to touch one of the articles. She just as quickly lowered her hand. "You followed my career," she breathed. "All of it."

"I did."

"Even though I'd given you no reason to hope."

He moved across the room to stand beside her. "I told myself I would stop doing this the day you married someone else." He slid an arm around her shoulders. "But you never seemed to have a serious boyfriend, so I kept this board going."

She wrinkled her nose up at him. "There were no boyfriends, serious or otherwise, Dev."

"Really?" He gazed in surprise down at her. "The media sure did some speculating from time to time." He remembered it all too well and the dread that had accompanied it.

She made a scoffing sound. "Ha! They'll sensationalize anything, even if it's not true." She held his gaze. "Which it wasn't."

He tapped her nose. "But you dated, right?"

Her cheeks turned pink. "Do I have to answer that?"

"Not if you don't want to."

"Oh, for crying out loud, Dev!" She rolled her eyes. "There was no one besides you. While you were canoodling with chickadees like Rosie McKeever, I was barrel racing and roping steers. Alone." She stabbed a finger at his chest. "Wishing you were there to cheer me on."

He caught her hand and held it against his heart, greatly humbled by her words. He'd admittedly allowed his anger and hurt to cloud his judgment where she was concerned, but he would gladly spend the rest of his life making it up to her if she'd let him.

There was no point in being anything but flat out honest with her. "Yes, I dated a few times, but only because I thought it was over between us. Nothing came of it."

She scowled at him. "Then why are there so many rumors flying around about you and Rosie?"

"I don't know." He shook his head in puzzlement.

"The day I arrived in town, word on the street was that you were about to propose to her."

"It was only one date. A quick meal at the diner." He grimaced at the memory, since it had ended in a rather bold move on Rosie's part. "Whether you returned to town or not, things would've never gone past the first date with her."

"Really? Because it ended in a pretty steamy kiss."

He felt his face turn red. "You heard about that, huh?" The memory still had the ability to make him cringe.

"Everybody in town heard about it, Dev. What's worse, I had to witness it."

His hand tightened over hers. "What are you talking about?"

"I was in the diner that day. I'd just returned to town. Rosie saw me. I assumed you did, too — that the kiss you shared with her was your way of punishing me."

"No!" He didn't realize how loud he'd spoken until she jumped. "Blast it all, Jules!" He threw his

Stetson on his desk to run a hand through his hair, hardly knowing what to say next. Catching her gaze again, he silently begged her to believe him. "If you were watching that closely, surely you saw I wasn't the one who initiated the kiss."

She shook her head. "I was beyond being objective at that point. I was too busy incinerating from the inside out."

He had no trouble getting the idea, since the hurt and betrayal she must have felt that day were still reflected in her gaze. Rage curled in his gut at the realization that someone had purposely put it there. "There was never anything serious between me and Rosie," he said flatly. "Asking her out was a mistake I would've never repeated. The rumors would have died a slow, painful death the way they always do in our small town."

A breathy chuckle escaped her. "Isn't that the truth!"

He laced his fingers through hers and held their joined hands over his heart. "Please assure me you understand what this board means, Jules." He angled his head at the shrine he'd built to her career, anxious to draw her attention back to the reason he'd brought her to his office.

Her shy smile chased away some of the hurt in her gaze. "It appears that you missed me while I was gone."

"Every blasted day!" His voice was ragged with emotion. "Whether you meant to or not, you took my heart with you on the road."

She turned impulsively to him, wrenching her hand from his in the process. "How ironic! I always felt like I left mine behind."

His pulse raced at her breathless tone. "Our hearts are together again. That's all that matters now." It was all that mattered to him, at any rate. He kept his hands at his side — waiting, hoping, and praying that she would choose him this time.

"Yes." She stepped closer to circle her arms around his middle and rest her head against his shoulder.

It was the word he'd waited eight years to hear. Joy shuddered through him as he absorbed the fact that she was finally his.

He tipped her chin up to his. "Say it again, Jules."

"Yes," she whispered. Her gaze was luminous with hope and a thousand unspoken promises.

In that moment, he finally understood the scripture in the Bible that said the greatest gift was love. Feeling like he'd been handed the world, he lowered his head over hers and tenderly covered her mouth with his.

Their kiss felt different this time. Newer. Fuller. Richer. Deeper. Stronger. They were no longer two high school kids caught in the throes of a wild attraction, trying to figure out what came next. They were adults now, who'd proven that none of their mistakes and mixed signals could snuff out a love as powerful as theirs.

CHAPTER 6: LONG OVERDUE

JULIA

Three days later

Julia awoke early to the sound of a man shouting. It was followed by the thunder of horse's hooves against the hard-packed ground.

Father? She tossed her blankets aside. Throwing her legs over the edge of the mattress, she felt around the floor with one bare foot for her shoes.

Locating a pair of flip-flops, she slipped her feet into them. She pulled a sweatshirt over the tank top and running shorts she'd slept in and shuffled to the bay window to peer outside.

And there he was.

Her father had one of the young quarter horses out in the training ring beside the barn. She recognized the spirited black creature. His name was Beast, and he was only seventeen months old, a little young to be saddle-broken just yet.

She watched in curiosity and growing concern as Cody Benson urged Beast to run around the ring. Why now? It was barely daybreak. Even from her second-story window, there was no missing how weary and winded her father looked, as if he was the one doing the running. Then he started to cough.

The horse jolted and yanked its head up, whinnying in alarm. He narrowly missed crashing into the fence and came to a standstill a few strides later. He stood here, pawing at the ground and bellowing in fear.

"That's it, mister! You're done!" Wondering if her father was losing his mind, Julia hobbled down the stairs as fast as she could. By the time she reached the bottom of the stairs, she was wishing she'd taken the time to wrap her sore knee. Good golly, but she'd probably be paying for it the rest of the day! It couldn't be helped, though. If her father was bent on losing life and limb outside this morning, it was up to her to stop him.

She limped across the front lawn, stubbing her toe on a paver stone she couldn't see in the dim light as she bypassed one of the flower beds.

"Ouch!" She yelled the word at the top of her lungs to warn her father of her pending approach.

His head whipped in her direction as she drew closer to the fence. His gaze narrowed on her limping gait. "What are you doing out here?"

"You woke me up with your bellowing," she retorted. Reaching the fence, she grasped it with both hands, leaning forward to take the weight off her aching knee. "What are *you* doing out here?"

"Training." He bit out the word and turned his back on her.

She strove to steady her voice. "Isn't he a little young?"

"Don't tell me how to run my business, kid."

Kid? "Well, pardon this kid for interfering. Guess I was just supposed to roll over and pretend I didn't hear you out here flushing your reputation as an award-winning trainer down the toilet?"

"That's enough, Julia!"

"Finally something we can agree on." With a huff of exertion that ended in a pained squeak, she vaulted over the fence. By some miracle, she landed on her good foot.

"Julia!" he roared, whirling angrily in her direction. He was immediately seized by another fit of coughing that made him nearly double over.

The quarter horse reared back, shrieking and pawing the air with his front hooves.

Fearful her father was about to be trampled, Julia wedged herself between the horse and him. "Whoa, boy!" The first command she issued was a sharp one, intended to get Beast's attention. Her second command was gentler. "Whoa, boy. Whooooooaaaaaa!" She drew out the word in a sing-song, seeking to calm him with her voice.

As she spoke, she shoved her hip against her father, nudging him backward one step at a time until both of them were out of striking range.

The horse bellowed out another complaint, then brought his hooves crashing back to the ground.

Julia continued to speak quietly until his nostrils stopped flaring in fear. "Good boy!" She wished she had a carrot or apple slice to offer him, but all she had was her presence. Holding out a hand to him, she slowly advanced on him. She stopped a few feet away and waited.

"I know you're afraid, but it's okay. No one is going to hurt you. That's a good boy. Very good boy."

After a tense few seconds of staring each other down, he slowly ambled her way to duck his nose against her hand.

"Good boy," she praised again, sliding her fingers down his silky nose. After she was sure the danger was past, she urged him toward the gate.

Her father was waiting for them there in stony silence. Beast balked a bit at the sight of him, but Julia sang and cooed him through his fright again.

The moment her father opened the gate, she led the horse through it, shooting a furious glare over her shoulder at him.

He closed the gate and followed at a distance as they made their way to the barn. Only after Julia had Beast tethered at the brushing station did her father approach them.

"You shouldn't have done that."

"Oh, I think that shoe is well on the other foot," she seethed, keeping her voice low. She didn't want to rile the horse all over again while she was brushing him down. "Did you forget you have pneumonia?"

"You won't let me forget," he snarled, slapping his riding crop against his jeans. "You follow me around with pill bottles and chicken soup, making me feel like a blasted invalid." Another fit of coughing interrupted his tirade.

She waited until he caught his breath. "Speaking of pill bottles, did you even bother to take your medicine this morning?"

His silence was telling.

"You have to take care of yourself if you plan on getting well, Dad."

He coughed some more, cleared his throat, and slapped his riding crop back on the shelf against the wall.

She watched him worriedly. "This isn't like you. You were so hard on me over the years, demanding nothing short of perfection when it came to horsemanship. That's why I don't understand where this is coming from." She gestured to Beast. "I've never seen you come this close to mistreating a horse." Something was wrong. She could sense it.

"Why do you even care, Julia?" Her father's voice was cold as he turned back to face her. "You took off and stayed gone eight miserable years. Did you come back just to torment me some more?" He took a step in her direction, lips parted as if planning on saying more. Then he stopped — stopped moving and stopped talking — as he waited for her to answer.

"Torment you?" If he was looking for a fight,

she'd be happy to give it to him. "Are you serious? All I've done is look after you since the moment I arrived home."

"I know," he roared. His face grew red. "The question is why?"

She was fast losing patience with his attitude. "Because I promised Mom I would!" The moment the words left her mouth, she realized her mistake.

The color left his face, and he swayed on his feet.

"Dad!" She dropped the brush and sprinted in his direction. By the time she reached him, her bad knee was buckling.

His arm shot out to catch her, while hers slid around his middle to catch him. They held onto each other for a dizzy moment. Then his forehead dropped to her shoulder.

"How long have you known she was alive?" He sounded strangely hoarse.

"Only a few weeks. What about you?" She didn't like the rattle she could feel in his chest as he drew a heaving breath.

"Your entire life, kid." His weight grew heavier as he slumped against her shoulders. For a moment, she feared he was going to pass out.

"Dad?" Her arms tightened around him. "Dad, listen to me. We've gotta get you inside, okay?"

He nodded wearily. Then he straightened. The next thing she knew, he was barking out an order to one of the ranch hands to tend Beast. Then he bent his knees to scoop her up in his arms.

"Dad!" she protested, hooking an arm around his broad shoulders.

He continued to trudge wordlessly with her to the house. He didn't set her down until they reached the back door. Even then, he remained in a stooped over position so she could keep her arm slung around his neck while he twisted the door open.

"Don't worry, kid. I've got you." He led her inside to the living room.

She allowed him to deposit her on the comfy leather sofa in the center of the room.

"Coffee?" he growled.

"Yes, please." She blinked at him in confusion, not understanding the change that had come over him. All she'd done was accidentally mention her mother, and boom! He'd turned into a different guy.

As he stomped and coughed his way to the kitchen, she called after him, "And take your stinking medicine already!" After he left the room, she added, "You hard-headed old goat!"

"I heard that," he muttered from the other side of the wall.

"No, you didn't," she returned sweetly.

He popped his head back around the doorway, coughing into his sleeve before responding. "You're just like her. You know that, right?"

She could only assume he was talking about her biological mother.

"Opinionated," he muttered. "Mouthy, bull-head-ed..." He finally left the room and returned a few minutes later to finish making the coffee. He shuffled her way, bearing two steaming mugs.

She accepted the one he offered her with a sigh of appreciation. "I love you, Dad."

He nearly dropped his cup. With a startled cough, he took a heavy seat on the cushion beside her and slung an arm across the back of the sofa behind her head. "You trying to give me a heart attack this morning?"

"No. I really do love you. At the moment, I don't care if you believe me." She was tired of all their verbal dueling, tired of playing games. She was tired all the way to her soul.

"I know you do, kid. Not sure I've given you a lot of reasons to, but—"

"You raised me," she interrupted fiercely. "You put bandaids on my boo-boos and read me bed-time stories. You made me do my homework, got me to soccer practice, and helped me pick out my prom dress. Shall I go on?"

"Nah." He shook his head, his jaw working with emotion. "I get it."

She twisted in her seat to face him. "I still need to know why you didn't tell me about Mom."

He exhaled heavily. "You do realize she faked her death?"

"Yeah. She told me, but she didn't say why." Julia scanned his haggard features. "Do you know why?"

"No." He shook his head. "I think her plan was for me to grieve and move on, which I did. Or tried to. When the Silver Streak hit the championship charts a year later, though, I figured out the truth."

Julia frowned at him. "What truth?"

"That she was still alive." His voice broke. "That she'd chosen to leave me." He swallowed with difficulty. "And give up our baby."

Julia reached out to touch his arm. "Dixie is convinced she had her reasons."

His tortured gaze met hers. "Who's Dixie?"

"Uncle Pete's wife, who also happens to be my realtor." At this point, Julia was very sure it was no coincidence that their paths had crossed.

"No kidding!" A shocked chuckle rumbled out of her father. "So, you know about Pete Flanagan, too?"

"Not much. All I really know is that Mom needed the money to bail him out of jail. Dixie thinks someone offered the funds in exchange for…" She bit her lower lip at the agony that leaped across her father's features. "I'm sorry, Dad. I truly am." She squeezed his forearm. "I can only imagine how hard it was for you to raise me alone." A sound of sympathy hummed out of her. "You've already pointed out how mouthy and opinionated I am."

"You were a real brat." His hard mouth twitched with humor. "But that wasn't the hard part." He sobered. "The hard part was watching your mom soar up the championship charts, knowing she'd chosen to be out there instead of here at home with us."

"Maybe she didn't have a choice," Julia mused, longing for answers.

"There's always a choice, kid." His voice was hard. "She didn't make the right one."

Julia grew still at the abject misery behind his words. "You loved her, didn't you?"

"Always and forever," he answered without hesitation. "Too bad she didn't feel the same way." He lifted red-rimmed eyes to her. "I'm sorry for not telling you. You had every right to know. Just couldn't bear the thought of my daughter knowing she had a mom out there who didn't want her. If that makes me a coward, then I'm a coward." He shrugged helplessly.

Julia scooted closer to him so she could lean against his side. "You're one of the strongest people I know."

"Does that mean you don't hate me for not telling you about your mom?" She'd never before heard so much uncertainty in his voice.

She lightly tapped a fist against his ribcage. "Thought I just finished telling you that I love you."

He drew a deep breath. "You spent most of your teen years acting like you hated me."

"Every teenager does that." She scowled at him. "I'll admit I wasn't too happy about you bringing home a stepmom."

"No kidding! I'd have never guessed." His voice was sarcastic as he tapped a callused finger against her nose.

"It's because I was so classy and subtle about it." She snuggled contentedly against him, happier than she'd been in a long time.

"Not even a little, you brat," he sighed, hitching her closer. "For what it's worth, I spent most of your childhood feeling guilty that you didn't have a mom in your life."

"You shouldn't have." Julia's voice was tart. "You were very good at being both a mom and a dad."

"How would you know, since you never had a mom?" he sighed.

She made a face that she hoped he didn't see. "How about I don't answer that question, and we can still be friends?"

"Oh, come on! Tonna wasn't that bad."

Julia could think of a few deer heads in the entry foyer that said otherwise, but she kept her silence.

"Julia!"

She gritted her teeth. "You did not simply get married for my sake. Just admit it already."

"I have no problem admitting that I was lonely."

"Please stop right there," she begged. "I don't want to have to wash out my ears with soap."

He snorted. "I waited a long time, kid. Years and years, hoping your mom would come home."

Julia suddenly straightened as an alarming thought hit her. "So, uh...I think that's exactly what she's planning on doing."

The shuttered expression on her father's face gave her pause. "You don't look surprised."

For an answer, he produced his cell phone, tapped on the screen, and handed it to her.

He'd pulled up a text message. It was from Brooke Flanagan.

"Mom texted you?" Julia breathed. Her hands started to shake with excitement as she cradled the phone and started reading.

I'm headed to Chipper tomorrow. —Silver Streak

"First time in twenty-five years." His voice was guarded. "Hard to believe she still has my number."

"It sounds like she knows that you know who she is." Saying the words felt a little like saying a tongue twister. "I think I said that right."

"She does. I'm not sure how, though." He waved a hand. "Maybe she saw me at one of her rodeo performances."

Julia's jaw dropped. "You went to *see* her?" *Holy smokes!* "When?"

He shook his head in self-recrimination. "Every chance I got."

It was obvious he still loved her mother. "Did, er…Tonna know?"

"I don't know." Her father fiddled with the handle of his coffee mug. "She wasn't too thrilled about the anonymous donation we received a few years back to finish paying off the mortgage on the ranch. I don't think she had any idea it was your mom, though."

"Oh, my lands, Dad!" Julia's mind raced as she assimilated everything she'd learned in the last few minutes. "So, Mom left us when I was a baby, bailed her brother out of jail, became a roaring success on the rodeo circuit, paid off the note on your ranch, and now she's coming back to Chipper. Am I missing anything?"

He sat forward, ducking his head over his coffee mug. "She's gonna turn this town upside-down, kid." He sounded winded again.

"Maybe it'll be a quick in-and-out." Julia returned his phone, setting it on his knee.

"My gut says otherwise." He closed a hand over his phone.

She touched his shoulder. "Are you okay?"

"No." Coughing into his sleeve, he stood.

She started to climb to her feet, but he turned around and pointed her back into her seat.

"Don't you dare! You've coddled me enough. It's my turn to take care of you."

———

Cody Benson didn't sleep that night. It felt like his brain was running a fever. He tossed and turned in his king-sized bed, knowing it had been years since anything had stirred him like this. Since he'd felt so angry. Or frustrated. Or stupidly happy. Just the thought of seeing Brooke again was making it harder to breathe.

He rolled onto his back and threw an arm across his eyes. As if he wasn't already having enough trouble breathing, thanks to the walking pneumonia that had been dragging on and on and on. He really hated the thought of her seeing him like this. Older. Weaker.

They'd dated back in his late teens and early twenties — when he was in his prime. And now he was forty-nine, pushing fifty. He had scarred and callused hands, a farmer's tan, and sun spots on his face. Though his body was still strong, he had more frost in his hair than he wanted and was in dire need of a haircut that he didn't have time to get today. Stifling a groan of self-pity, he made his way to the master bathroom to splash water on his face. He straightened and stared at himself in the mirror. Nothing but a dim nightlight glowed in the room, casting his face in the shadows. It lent his features an almost demonic cast.

Yeah, I'm a real catch. That's why the single women were lined up at his door...not! For reasons he chose not to analyze too closely, he took another shower, shaved, and put on a new shirt. Not that anyone would notice. He pretty much only wore plaid button-up shirts. He also brushed and flossed his teeth and administered a single spritz of cologne.

If Julia noticed, she'd dog him endlessly about it. All he cared about, though, was not looking as sick as a dog the first time Brooke laid eyes on him again.

He felt better today, for whatever that was worth. He wasn't sure why since he hadn't slept a wink, but he wasn't complaining. Maybe the meds were finally working. Maybe he'd finally turned that blasted corner.

Julia already had the coffee brewing when he made it to the kitchen. "Did you wrap your knee?" he barked.

"Yes," she barked back, raising her chin at him. "Did you take your prescription meds?"

"Yep." He reached for the coffee she was handing him.

She held onto the cup a few seconds longer than necessary, sniffing the air curiously.

"Don't say it," he growled. He had no interest in explaining why he was wearing cologne this morning.

"Okay, but I'm thinking it." She grinned and took a sip of her own coffee.

He leaned back against the cabinet, trying to think of a way to push the conversation ball back to her. "Anything new going on between you and that Cassidy boy?"

She shrugged. "We kiss," she informed him with the mischievous glint he couldn't get enough of. It reminded him so poignantly of her mother. "A lot."

"I get it. Talking about your boyfriend is off-limits. See?" He waved a hand with mock cheerfulness. "I can take a hint."

"No, you can't." She made a face at him. "And we really do kiss a lot." She took a noisy sip of coffee, probably just to annoy him.

He slurped his coffee even louder than she had. "So, you really are back together?"

"Yep."

He lowered his mug, studying her with concern. "Are you happy?"

"I am." She smiled cheekily at him over the top of her mug.

"Good. Then maybe I won't have to shoot him." He took one final sip before setting his half-full mug on the cabinet. With a wink at her, he strode from the room to collect his Stetson from the hall tree. Whistling, he exited through the side door and took the porch steps two at a time.

He felt a little guilty about not telling Julia about the conversation he'd had with her mother last night. Every word of it was seared into his memory. In the middle of the night, he'd swallowed his pride and texted her back.

When can I see you?

Her reply had nearly sent him into cardiac arrest. *I'll be serving breakfast at the homeless shelter.* Talk about making an entrance! When the citizens of Chipper found out they had a celebrity barrel racer serving soup and bread to the poorest among them, there was no telling how many television cameras would come rolling her way.

He could only hope he reached her first. They needed to talk. Man, but they needed to talk!

His heart pounded during the entire drive to the shelter. It was nestled between an old abandoned warehouse and a newer grocery store. The short, squatty red-brick building came with no extra frills. No fancy signs. No flower pots. Just a simple white poster taped inside the front window with two words written on it: *Free Breakfast*.

A silver fifth wheel was hitched to a sleek red dual-cab F-150 at the far end of the parking lot. It was a long, custom trailer. The back half of it boasted a series of windows, most of which were pushed open. He could hear the whinny of a horse from within.

It had to be hers. It just had to be. He watched as a uniformed groom appeared with a bale of hay in one hand and a bucket in the other.

"Can I help you?"

Cody was surprised to hear a voice at his elbow. He'd been too busy scrutinizing the fifth wheel to hear anyone approach.

Glancing over at the owner of the voice, he found himself staring at a dark-skinned man in dark sunglasses. He was wearing a navy business suit. An earpiece with a clear spiral cord wound its way beneath the collar of his white dress shirt.

Cody shrugged. "I'm Cody Benson, here to meet—"

"Come with me," the man in the suit interrupted.

To Cody's surprise, he was escorted straight to the door of the silver trailer.

The man opened it for him and ushered him up the short flight of steps. "She's expecting you, sir."

"Thanks." Huffing out a resigned breath, Cody squared his shoulders and entered the trailer. It took a moment for his vision to adjust to the dim interior.

The first thing that became apparent was the scent of pumpkin pie baking. It was his favorite. He pressed a hand to his chest at the realization that she'd remembered. Also to hold back the cough that was working its way up his throat.

The next thing that became apparent was the woman seated at a table in front of him.

"Hello, Cody." It was the Silver Streak. The

mother of his child. The woman he'd never stopped loving.

The knowledge made his knees weak.

Her face paint was missing this morning. There was nothing to mask the deep blue of her questioning gaze or the tiny lines at the edges of her eyes. She was wearing her blonde hair down this morning. It cascaded around the shoulders of her fringed blue shirt, which was tucked into a waistline as slender as the day they'd met. No one would ever guess that the whip-thin woman had ever given birth to a child — *his* child. The realization that she was exactly what Julia would look like twenty years from now made his heart tighten with emotion.

She waved at the empty cushioned bench across from her. He took a seat, grateful to take a load off. The walking pneumonia had weakened him. He got tired a lot quicker these days.

"Say something," she pleaded, pushing a white porcelain cup his way.

He barely looked at it. He was too busy searching her lovely features for answers. She was even more beautiful now. The discovery shook him.

He opened his mouth and tried to speak, but no sound came out. Shaking his head, he tried again, hating how damp his eyes grew as he spoke.

"Why, Brooke? Just tell me why."

CHAPTER 7: SMALL TOWN SCANDAL
DEVLIN

One week later

The jingle of the front doorbell made Dev's head swivel toward it. His heart sank at the sight of the woman gliding into the store.

Rosie McKeever's light brown hair was tossed by the wind, lending a girlish innocence to her appearance. He knew from personal experience that she was anything but. She was wearing super short cutoff jean shorts and high-heeled boots that further underscored the shortness of her shorts.

"And people wonder why I'm still single," Emerson muttered, joining him behind the counter that housed the cash register. "Bro, you gotta leave something to a guy's imagination."

Dev couldn't have agreed more, though all he did was reach for the nearest crate of fresh produce. It was fall, and the harvest was plentiful. Cassidy Farm was practically bursting with this year's crop of pumpkins, zucchini, squash, beets, and carrots. Plus, there were Brussels sprouts, broccoli, potatoes, cauliflower, cucumbers, radishes, and bush beans. Though he'd packed away two sandwiches for lunch, it made him hungry just sorting the vegetables. He placed them artfully in cardboard cartons, getting them ready to put on display.

Emerson grabbed a second set of cardboard cartons and helped him with the sorting. Dev suspected his twin was watching their latest customer covertly, the same as he was. The fact that she remained in their direct line of sight felt deliberate. So did all her stretching to reach high shelves and bending to reach lower shelves.

"Shallow." Emerson snickered. "Bro, what did you ever see in her?"

"Nothing. I was only trying to forget someone else." Dev was past the point of pretending his heart had ever belonged to anyone besides Julia. "Didn't work."

"Speaking of things that work," Emerson sang out cheerfully. He was careful to keep his voice down so that the two of them were the only ones who could hear what he said. "You've been a lot happier since a certain barrel racer returned to town."

"What can I say? She makes me happy." Dev juggled three yellow squash to emphasize his point.

Emerson snatched one of the gourds out of the air. "Hey! There's no need to rub my nose in it. Some of us are still single and miserable, in case you've forgotten."

"Really?" Dev caught the other two squash and tucked them carefully into a display carton. "Because as much as you enjoy complaining about your single-ness, you never seem in short supply of female companionship."

"Only because I'm a friendly guy." Emerson play-fully stuck out his chest. "It's not the same as being annoyingly in love like the rest of my brothers."

"Oh, don't worry. You've got the annoying part down to a T," Dev assured blandly. "Enough to give Fox a run for his money."

"Now you're just being insulting." Emerson scowled at him.

"And here I thought I was being subtle." Dev finished filling two cartons with vegetables and reached for two more empty cartons. "Last I heard, Fox was still single, too, so you're not the only one wallowing in single-hood."

His twin looked down his nose at him. "Are you truly that uninformed?"

"I'm not uninformed." Dev tweaked a dead leaf off a pumpkin stem and tossed it his way. "I'm well aware that Fox has dated every female within a hundred-mile radius. I've never seen him serious about anyone, though. Does he even do second dates?"

"Wow! You're on a roll with the hilariousness." Emerson slapped away the leaf. "Fox is just hard to please. It's like he's holding out for royalty or something."

"Speaking of royalty," Dev tossed another dead

leaf his twin's way, "what's this I hear about you inviting Miss Texas to serve as our master of ceremonies at the next rodeo?"

Emerson shrugged like it was no big deal. "She and I met during my last bronc riding event. She was rodeo queen at the Houston Livestock Show and Rodeo. We've stayed in touch, and—"

"Whoa!" The details finally clicked into place for Dev. "So, that's why you've been all hot and bothered lately about tightening your pecs and sculpting your biceps, eh?"

To his disappointment, Emerson was barely listening. Either that, or he was pretending not to hear in order to avoid answering the question. His attention was back on Rosie, who was prancing in their direction. "Load the potato guns, boys, and prepare for battle."

"Don't I wish," Dev grumbled, bracing himself for an awkward encounter. He'd been avoiding Rosie ever since she'd kissed him at the diner. "Listen, I've got this. You should probably head back over to the bakery counter." He was surprised his twin had left it unattended for this long already.

"Not happening, bro."

Before Dev could formulate a comeback, Rosie pounced on them.

"Hey, Dev!" She tumbled an armful of honey products on the counter.

"Hi, Rosie." He kept his voice noncommittal. "Hope you found everything you're looking for."

"Mostly." She made a pouty face, flicking a

handful of hair over her shoulder. "I could really use your opinion on one thing, though." She held out her wrist to him. "I'm trying to figure out which of these lotions smell the best on me. Here's the first one."

He stared blankly at her outstretched arm, then at his twin, silently begging to be rescued.

"Uh...so, ah..." Emerson bobbed his head closer to Rosie's arm to give it a quick sniff. "My evil twin has been exposed to the Bubonic plague. Trust me. You don't want his schnozzle anywhere near you right now."

Dev snorted. "It was pneumonia, actually."

Rosie's smile slipped. "You mean the Bensons?"

Emerson cocked his thumb and forefinger at her. "Bingo."

She rolled her eyes. "Omigosh! Can you believe the whole return-from-the-dead act Brooke Flanagan is playing with him? I'm so not buying her sudden interest in being a parent, no matter how much charity work she does."

"Whoa, there! Time out!" Emerson held up his hands like a referee. "None of us knows the whole story."

"I don't need the whole story," Rosie spat. "Any woman who'll dump a newborn baby on a man to raise by himself—"

"About that lotion you were asking our opinion on," Dev interrupted, hoping like crazy to change the subject. *I should've just let the Bubonic plague story ride!* It was his fault for bringing up the topic of pneumonia. He'd unwittingly provided the perfect segue to the biggest scandal that had ever rocked their small town.

"Oh, for pity's sake!" Rosie made a face at him. "Just ring 'em both up. You know me. It'll take me weeks to decide if your mom's latest masterpiece is my new favorite scent."

Whereas it probably took you less than five minutes to condemn Brooke Flanagan to eternal damnation. Dev struggled to keep his expression neutral. "Let me know what you decide, and I'll be happy to pass the word on to my mom. She appreciates the feedback."

She nodded, making a clucking sound under her breath. "Sorry for getting so steamed about the Flanagan woman. I just feel so sorry for Cody Benson. It's like the females in his life are good at one thing only — leaving."

That wasn't entirely true, considering both Julia and Brooke had recently returned to town, but Dev didn't see any good in pointing that out. While he and Emerson rang up Rosie's purchases, they were forced to endure several more minutes of nonstop criticism from her.

"Maybe she'll find some sort of redemption by serving food to the homeless. That said, people aren't going to forget what she's done. It's a good thing she's already made a name for herself. Otherwise, this would ruin her career."

Both Dev and Emerson nodded and made occasional noises that she seemed to interpret as agreement, since she kept up her babbling. "I mean really!

There are consequences for stuff like that, and she'll be paying them for the rest of her life."

Five minutes earlier

Julia turned into the parking lot of the Cassidy Farm store a little faster than she should have and skidded a little on the gravel. She giggled as she feathered her brakes, hoping no one had seen her. The guilt she felt over the cloud of dust her tires stirred up was tempered with the joy of knowing she was about to pay an impromptu visit with Dev.

She was happier than she'd been in a long time. Not only was her relationship with her dad improving, she was also making slow but steady progress easing her way back into the good graces of the locals. Not only had she sold her third sponsorship this morning for the signage at her future racetrack, she'd also managed to reserve a big equipment operator and his team to start leveling and grading her property right after lunch. She was dying to celebrate, and her boyfriend's family just happened to own and operate a bakery that served up the most divine sweets. Plus, it was on the way to where she was going.

She glanced at her watch. It was a quarter 'til noon. That meant she might actually catch Dev before he took his lunch break. If she was really lucky, she might be able to join him on his lunch break before having to head back out to meet the grading crew.

The thought excited her so much that she jammed on her brakes and skidded her way into the parking spot next to Dev's pickup truck.

"Oops," she muttered. "I did it again." A shiver of movement to her right caught her attention. A quick glance through the passenger window verified that her latest sin had been witnessed by none other than Claire Cassidy herself. Dev's mother was hurrying her way — determined, it seemed, to seek an audience with her.

Guess I better apologize. Julia pushed her door open and hopped to the ground to face the petite blonde woman in jeans. "I'm so sorry about skidding through your parking lot." She offered the woman an apologetic smile.

Claire Cassidy stared at her in surprise. Then she slapped the air. "As the mother of six boys, I am well accustomed to screeching and skidding tires, donuts in the parking lot, and drag races on the highway out yonder. What little you did isn't even worth mentioning. Trust me."

Julia giggled. "Thanks. I'm still sorry for skidding in your parking lot — not once, but twice. I've had such a good morning that I'm afraid I went a little heavy on the gas pedal."

"Oh?" Mrs. Cassidy brushed a wisp of hair from her cheek, looking interested.

"Yeah, I just finished securing an equipment crew to start leveling a piece of land," Julia babbled without thinking. Then she stopped, realizing that her news would mean nothing without a lot more context. Unsure what all Dev had told his parents yet about her racetrack project, she sought to change the subject. "To be honest, I was mainly looking for an excuse to go indulge in one of y'all's signature lattes."

Smiling in appreciation, Mrs. Cassidy unlocked the rear door of the barn store and ushered Julia in ahead of her. "If you want to take a shortcut to the bakery, head straight down the hall and take the last door on the left. I'd offer to join you if I didn't have such a tall stack of vendor receipts to enter into the log books." Her smile was rueful. "I'm not complaining, though. God is good, and business is booming."

"I'm glad to hear it." Julia skipped through the open door. "Thanks for the shortcut," she tossed over her shoulder.

"No problem." Mrs. Cassidy made a scoffing sound. "You're practically family."

"Thank you." It warmed Julia's heart to hear those words. Once upon a time, she'd been like family to the Cassidys. With all the water under the bridge, though, she hadn't been sure if they still felt that way about her. She slowed her steps, wanting to say more but not sure exactly what to say.

Claire Cassidy nodded in quiet understanding. "I'm glad you're home. It's where you belong."

Home. Julia blinked back the sting of tears, reveling in the warmth and acceptance in the woman's voice. "It's good to be back, ma'am."

Claire ducked inside the nearest office, then popped her head back around the door. "If you're in the mood to be kind to a woman who's about to be up to her neck in paperwork, bring me something to drink on your way out."

"Of course!" Julia was thrilled to be asked. "What would you like?"

"Surprise me, sweetie." Claire disappeared inside the office.

Julia smiled all the way to the bakery door, twisted the handle, and let herself into the dining area. To her surprise, neither Emerson nor Dev were manning the counter. It looked like the customers who were seated had already been served. They were chatting with friends, munching on kolaches, and sipping coffee.

Grinning, she considered walking up to the counter and tapping the bell a few times just to be annoying. It would be fun to see which brother came running first.

A quick glance across the store, however, made her stiffen. It was no wonder the bakery was currently unmanned. Both Cassidy twins were standing behind the main cash register counter, talking to none other than Rosie McKeever.

Julia inwardly cringed when the woman leaned across the counter and held up her wrist to Dev's nose. She could only assume Rosie was trying to get him to sniff her perfume or something. It was a ridiculously intimate request to make of someone else's boyfriend.

She was openly flirting with him. There was no other way to describe the coy little smiles she kept sending his way or how far she was leaning across the counter.

Deciding a little intervention might be in order, Julia glided their way, inwardly debating the best way to make her presence known. As she neared the counter, her stomach tightened to discover that the topic of their conversation was none other than Brooke Flanagan!

"Maybe she'll find some sort of redemption by serving food to the homeless," Rosie proclaimed in a self-righteous voice. "That said, people aren't going to forget what she's done. It's a good thing she's already made a name for herself. Otherwise, this could ruin her career."

Julia's lips parted in indignation as she watched both Dev and Emerson nod their heads and make occasional noises that could be interpreted as anything. No, they weren't outright agreeing with the woman, but they weren't exactly leaping to Julia's mother's defense, either.

"I mean really," Rosie babbled. She turned her head in what felt like a deliberate movement as she glanced over at Julia and caught her eye. "There are consequences for stuff like that, and she'll be paying them for the rest of her life," she finished in a smug voice.

Her superior smile made Julia want to gnash her teeth. Instead, she bit her lower lip. "Hey, Rosie. Hey, Dev and Emerson." It wasn't near as fun as ringing the bakery bell would've been, but she stepped up to the counter to slap her hands down on it. "What's it gonna take to get some service over by the coffee machine?"

Rosie's lower lip came out in what Julia could only presume was supposed to be a simpering pout. "Hey! No cutting in line."

"Oh, come on! It's clearly a separate line over there." Julia tossed her ponytail, trying like crazy to hang onto the last thread of her temper before it snapped. She faced Dev and strove to adopt a playful voice. "Two lines and two Cassidy brothers."

Rosie's gasp of outrage assured Julia that her jibe had hit home. "You know what? Some of us actually work for a living." She turned her back on Julia. "So, if you'll just finish ringing me up…" Her tone of voice insinuated that no one else's schedule was half as important as hers.

Smirking, Emerson finished scanning her purchases, and Rosie stomped from the store. She gave the Cassidy brothers a simpering wave, but completely ignored Julia.

After the door shut behind her, Dev leaned his elbows on the counter and reached for Julia's hands. "I feel like I've been run over by a train."

"Not sure why." She scowled at him. "It sounded more like my mother was the one being driven over when I walked up."

"Eh, sorry you had to hear that." Dev lifted her right hand to his mouth to kiss her fingers. "Rosie was gunning for a fight that we didn't give her."

With a snicker, Emerson broke into a comical imitation of their recently departed customer. *"People will never forget."* He had to pinch his nostrils together to produce a nasal voice. "I think she's greatly underestimating the capacity folks have for kindness in this town."

"And forgiveness," Dev agreed. "If Rosie continues down that path, she might find herself on the outside looking in at some point."

Realizing that Dev and Emerson were on her side, after all, went a long way toward unruffling Julia's feathers. As much as she would've loved to have seen one of them sock Rosie in the nose, it was better to have kept the peace. She was a little shamefaced, in hindsight, for the verbal dig she'd sent Rosie's way.

Dev toyed idly with her fingers for a moment, his expression serious. "I've lost count of the number of times I've personally screwed up and needed forgiveness. Guess we all need a little grace now and then."

"Isn't that the truth?" she said softly. "Thanks for being so understanding about my mom. It means a lot."

His hand tightened on hers. "Welcome. And I really am sorry you overheard Rosie's outburst of small-mindedness. If we'd have realized you were in the room, we'd have hustled her out the door all the sooner."

"Thanks." Julia smiled her gratitude at him. "So, er, before I forget, I promised your mom I'd bring her a drink from the bakery. She's back in the office, doing paperwork."

"What about you?" Dev searched her face as he straightened. "Have you had lunch yet?"

"I…" She was no longer hungry. "I'm actually on my way to meet the company I just hired to start leveling my property."

"That's great news!" Dev held on to her hand as he made his way around the counter, towing her along with him. "Let me at least fuel you up with some coffee and eats."

She eyed him guiltily, not feeling like she deserved his kindness at the moment. She wished she'd kept driving, instead of stopping by the store. "Listen, I'm sorry for losing my temper with Rosie."

Dev rolled his eyes. "She had it coming."

"It's still no excuse." Julia bit her lip, hating to admit — even to herself — that Rosie had been right about at least one thing. *You reap what you sow.* Julia decided on the spot that she was going to extend an olive branch to the woman the next time she ran into her.

"Alright, then." Without warning, Dev whisked her behind a row of shelves. "If you really have to dash, just promise me this."

"What?" Before she could take a breath, his mouth lightly brushed hers.

"Date night. Tonight. I'll pick you up at seven."

"I'm in!" As she kissed him back, her spirits picked up again at the realization that she was truly dating an amazing guy.

————

Two hours later

Julia leaned against the side of her Jeep, feeling glum. The guy with the tractor crew she'd hired to come level and grade her land was nearly two hours late. He wasn't responding to any of her texts or phone messages, either. It was as if he'd dropped off the face of the earth. It was way too bad he'd required a fifty percent down payment on the job. She was starting to wonder if she'd been scammed.

The sound of an approaching vehicle gave her pause. Glancing up hopefully, her heart sank all over again at the shiny red F-150 rumbling her way. Not that she wasn't glad to see her mother, but she would've preferred to see a fleet of tractors right now. A cloud of smoke rose from the gravel in the truck's wake.

Her mother pulled in behind Julia's Jeep and parked. Her slender frame leaped down from the driver's seat seconds later. A long, blonde ponytail swung around her shoulders, slapping against the arm of her fringed denim shirt.

"Hey, hon!" Shielding her eyes from the sun, Brooke Flanagan reached back inside her truck to grab a Stetson. She perched it on her head and adjusted her ponytail. Instead of immediately approaching her daughter's side, however, she seemed to be waiting for something.

When the passenger door of the truck opened,

Julia realized what the holdup was. Her father climbed down, keeping a cell phone balanced between his shoulder and ear. He was talking to someone on the phone.

Julia wasn't sure what her parents were doing here, much less what they were doing here together. She'd informed them she'd be busy all day with the ground leveling project, probably tomorrow, too. That's what she'd believed to be true, at any rate. It looked like she'd been wrong.

As her parents approached, Julia folded her arms and glumly regarded the empty field in front of them. "Don't ask."

"Wasn't going to." Her mother leaned against the Jeep beside her. "We came to deliver a message." She watched Julia's father approach.

Though he was still on the cell phone, he nodded at Julia. Then his gaze settled on Brooke and stayed there. They seemed to be exchanging some sort of silent message.

They were acting kind of strange, come to think of it. Julia hoped they hadn't come to deliver more bad news. She wasn't in the mood. "Please tell me it involves ice cream. According to Dad, ice cream makes everything better."

Her mother smiled at him from beneath her lashes. "Far be it for me to criticize the parenting skills of the man who did such an amazing job raising our daughter, but…"

As he ended his phone call, there was a dangerous glint in his eyes. The glint softened with affection as he caught the last of what Brooke said. He waggled his eyebrows playfully at her. "There's always a *but* with you, woman."

Looking sublimely innocent, she held up her hands in defense. "Y'all are more than welcome to your ice cream. I wasn't trying to rain on a hallowed family tradition."

"You could prove it by joining us," her father challenged.

Julia stared in amazement at her parents, wondering what was going on. It had been a rough afternoon, so maybe she was mistaken, but it was starting to sound like they were flirting.

"So, here's the deal." Brooke Flanagan abruptly returned her attention to her daughter. "Cody ran inside a service station earlier to grab a coffee refill, and he overheard a certain local citizen bragging to a few other local citizens about how it would be a cold day in Disney World before he, well, did what you were paying him to do out here." She waved a hand at the empty field in front of them. "He made noises about some sort of breach of contract and acted like he was going to simply pocket your fifty percent down payment and walk away. Fortunately, your dad was there to set him straight."

She reached inside the pocket of her jeans. "Under the threat of our family going public with his poor business practices on social media, he wrote out a check on the spot." She waved it in front of her daughter.

Julia accepted it and read the amount. It was a full

reimbursement for the down payment. "Oh, sheesh!" Her shoulders sagged in relief. "How can I ever thank you?"

"By allowing your dad to help select the next construction crew." Brooke's mouth tightened in a determined line. "He's handled his fair share of bullies over the years, hon, and he's more than willing to help out on the contracting side of things. At least, until you get your sea legs under you."

"Willing, huh?" Julia couldn't have been more thrilled about her father's interest in her current business venture. Originally, she hadn't been sure he'd approve. She probably had Brooke Flanagan to thank for that. "I take it he's willingly playing the part of bodyguard this afternoon, too?" Glancing around the vehicle, she didn't see any of the usual suits hovering around her mother.

"Yes." Her mom sent her dad a grateful look. "Since this isn't Dallas, Chicago, or Las Vegas, we thought we'd try something a little lower profile and see how it works."

Julia's eyes widened in amazement. *Way to go, Dad!* He gave her a slight head shake, which she understood to mean he didn't want her to make a big deal out of it. "As long as he keeps you safe, I approve."

He curled his upper lip at her. "If you say one blasted thing about my blasted meds, kid…"

She burst out laughing. "I wasn't going to. Now that you've brought it up, though, I'll say this. You look like you're feeling better."

"Probably because today is the last day I have to take those stupid pills," he conceded.

Julia wasn't so sure that completing his latest round of meds was the only reason he was feeling better, but she let it ride. He'd been through a lot. They all had. Despite his widower status, however, he now had his daughter back in his life, along with the first woman he'd ever loved — a woman he still loved. Both of those things were probably contributing to his recovery.

"Confession time." Julia stuffed the reimbursement check into her back pocket. "I've struck out with the rest of these local contractors. Everybody is either booked through the next century, has broken down equipment, or isn't interested in having a racetrack built in Chipper." She shook her head. "They sure don't hold back sharing their opinions on the subject."

Her father rested his hands on his hips as he assessed the area needing to be leveled. "I've located a crew in Amarillo that's willing to drive down here. They're bonded, insured, have plenty of online reviews, and a buddy of mine works there."

"I'm interested." Julia pushed away from her Jeep to throw her arms around him. "When can they start?"

"Right away, actually. Some holdup with a building permit on one of their other projects has freed up one of his crews for a few days."

She stared at him in amazement. "Looks like our ice cream date is on me."

"I accept." He enclosed her in a bear hug. Speaking over the top of her head, he inquired, "You in, Brooke?"

"I'm in, Cody."

The warmth in her mother's voice made Julia blink against her father's shoulder. Yeah, something was definitely going on between the two of them.

―――――

Julia left the diner early, claiming she had a date with Dev to get ready for. Cody didn't know if it was true, or if his daughter was slyly making herself scarce so he could be alone with Brooke. Either way, he was grateful.

They were seated across from each other at the booth. His appetite hadn't fully returned after the pneumonia, so he was having a hard time finishing his ice cream cone. He was giving it the ol' college try, though.

Without warning, Brooke reached across the table and snatched his half-eaten cone from him. Propping it inside her empty coffee mug, she declared, "You're done. Let's go."

He was a little disappointed that she was cutting their visit short. He'd been enjoying her company. However, he nodded and slid off the vinyl bench, tossing a tip on the table.

She stepped closer to him in the aisle of the crowded diner to murmur beneath her breath. "It feels like everyone in the room is staring at us."

"Because they are." He'd noticed it, too. Angling his head toward the front door, he ushered her forward. Or tried to.

She spun around to face him, stepping directly into his path as he started moving. His hands came up to clutch her upper arms, as much to steady himself as to avoid body slamming her.

To his amazement, she momentarily leaned into him, resting her cheek against his chest. "That's better," she sighed, giving him a hug. It was another few seconds before she dropped her arms and started walking again.

A murmur rose around them as they exited the restaurant.

"What was that all about?" He kept a hand on her elbow as he led her to her truck.

"What do you mean?" Her voice was innocent.

"You know what I mean." Feeling bold, he led her to the driver's side instead of the passenger side and assisted her up. Other than when he'd been negotiating grading contracts on the phone earlier, she usually preferred him to drive.

She shimmied over a little but remained in the center of the seat. "They were already talking about us, Cody."

"I am aware." He slid into the seat beside her. "Seems to me you gave them a little more to talk about tonight."

"Did I?"

Heart pounding, he drove in silence back to her silver trailer at the campgrounds. His truck was parked next to it. Though it was a tight squeeze, he edged her F-150 into the slot beside his.

The silence was starting to wear on his nerves. He wished she'd say something. When she didn't, he turned impulsively to her. "Brooke, what are we doing?"

She gave him a tight smile. "I thought you were driving me back to my trailer."

That wasn't what he was talking about, and she knew it. He stubbornly held her gaze. "What do you want from me? For real?" Life was too short, and they were too old for games.

"Everything." Though her eyes grew damp, her voice was fierce. "I came to town for one reason only — to beg your forgiveness. The experts say it's part of the healing process. But now that I'm here, I find myself wanting more. Things I can never have, but that doesn't keep me from wanting them." She twisted her hands in her lap as the words tumbled out of her. "I want the years back that I forfeited with you and Julia. I want to be the mother I never was, the woman I wasn't capable of being back then…"

Cody strained closer to her, longing to hear anything that would indicate she missed being in his life, as well.

She sniffled loudly. "But there's no going back, is there?"

"No." His heart clenched. "I've always preferred going forward, though." Her face blurred a little as he settled back against the seat cushion. Finding out the truth about why she'd left them hadn't been easy.

She'd finally come clean with him about being a closet alcoholic most of her life, including her bout of postpartum depression. His parents had discovered it and offered to send her to rehab. In a drunken rage, Brooke had instead negotiated the payment of her brother's bail bond in exchange for leaving town. The whole faking-her-own-death shenanigans had been yet another one of her drunken brainstorms.

Everyone involved in the exchange had been wrong, of course. Though Brooke had acted irresponsibly as a new parent, Cody's parents should've never interfered in their lives. They should've come to him about her drinking problem. She should've had the chance to receive proper medical care.

"Please tell me you understand I would've destroyed you if I'd stayed in town." Brooke's voice shook.

A pained breath eased out of him. "I don't think there's any way to Monday morning quarterback something like this."

"What if I'd have hurt Julia?" Tears gushed down Brooke's cheeks. "What if I'd dropped her, or…or…"

Cody reached for her hand to stop her self-flagellation. "Like I said, the only direction to go from here is forward."

She nodded, swallowing hard. "What if, um…I'm not ready to leave town yet?"

"Then don't." He curled his fingers more firmly around hers. If she was looking for permission from him, she had it.

"Are you sure you don't mind?" Her voice was

ragged. "I know I don't have any right to show up like this after Julia is all grown up."

"It's a free country, Brooke." He knew she was only repeating what the gossips were saying, but he couldn't have disagreed more. As far as he was concerned, the mother of his child could stay in Chipper as long as she wanted with his blessing.

"I'm trying to be considerate of you," she whispered, anxiously scanning his features.

The longing to kiss her slammed into him so powerfully that all he could do was breathe through it for a few seconds. When he finally found his voice again, he drawled, "Just for the record, I kind of like having you around." It was an understatement of horrendous proportions. The truth was that he loved having her around and couldn't bear the thought of her leaving again. Ever.

"If I stay, they're going to talk about us, Cody." Brooke's smile was sad.

His eyebrows rose. "Uh, newsflash. They're going to talk about us no matter what."

"I'm sorry for throwing more fuel on that fire tonight."

He snorted. "You didn't seem sorry earlier."

She blushed. "Sometimes I do awful things when I'm angry.

"Really? I hadn't noticed."

She used their joined hands to shove at his chest. "Don't be a jerk."

He drew back in mock offense, tugging her playfully closer in the process. "I thought you liked it."

"I do," she confessed breathlessly. "I always have." She wrinkled her nose at him. "Another one of my many weaknesses."

He slowly dipped his head closer to hers. "If you don't want this, tell me to stop."

"I do want it." She reached up to press her fingers to his lips to stop his advance. "Just not tonight. Not like this." A fresh wave of tears glistened in her eyes.

He drew back with a weary expulsion. "What did I do wrong this time?"

"Nothing. I just promised myself I wouldn't make the same old mistakes." Her furtive glance at the backseat was his first clue as to what she was worried about.

"Ditto." He shook his head sadly, remembering how their daughter had been conceived. Neither of them had been fully sober that night. "I've done a lot of things wrong, too, Brooke. This isn't all on you."

Her lashes grew damp from the weight of the tears yet to fall. "It's pretty huge of you to say that."

"It's true, and you know it. I'm not going to let you carry that alone."

She blinked rapidly and dabbed at the dampness that escaped the corners of her eyes. "What if we take things slow this time and try really hard to do them in the right order?"

"I'd like that." *A lot.* Hope tugged at his chest, lifting it and erasing the heaviness. "Where do we start?"

"At a spot you're not going to like."

"Oh?" Man, but he'd missed this! Brooke was

forever saying and doing the unexpected, keeping him on his toes. He was never bored around her.

"Come to church with me on Sunday, Cody."

Oh, boy! He drank in her pleading expression. In that moment, he realized how much she'd truly changed — how hard she was trying to be the best version of herself. And he knew with sudden certainty that things were only going to get better from here. If that meant he had to get his own act together, then so be it. Their family was worth it. She was worth it.

"Okay." He pushed open the truck door. Reaching back inside, he assisted her to the ground.

"That's it?"

"Yep."

She made a face. "I figured a reprobate like you would at least put up a fight."

"Is that so?" He cupped her cheek, dragging his thumb tenderly along the underside of her chin. "You obviously have no idea how bad I want to kiss you again."

"Cody," she murmured. Her gaze shimmered with wonder.

"'Night, Brooke." He dropped his hand and waited beside his truck until she'd safely locked herself in her trailer. He drove away whistling.

CHAPTER 8: DATE NIGHT

JULIA

Julia headed home to shower and change, more than a little shaken up over everything that had happened today. She'd done her best to hide it from her parents, but she was still upset over a few things. No, at her age, ice cream did *not* make everything better.

Though she was grateful for the support of her mom and dad, along with the three business owners who'd purchased signage space for her future stadium, there'd been too much bad mixed with the good. Today had not turned out to be the big success she'd originally thought it was going to be. It felt more like two steps forward and three steps back.

Rosie McKeever clearly had it out for the Bensons and Flanagans. She wasn't even trying to hide her venom. She was so outspoken, in fact, that Julia had to wonder how many more of the locals shared her opinions. The equipment operator who'd stood her up was in that camp for sure.

It was downright discouraging to know that she was in the process of trying to build a business in this town. Would the good ever outweigh the bad, or would she end up regretting her decision to return to Chipper in the long run?

Some of what she was feeling must've been stamped across her features when Dev drove up to the front of the house. He kept his truck motor idling as he hopped down to assist her up into the seat. Though she pasted a smile on her face as she accepted his help, he took one look at her face and scowled. "What's wrong?"

"Ouch!" She pretended to misunderstand. "Is that your way of saying you don't like my dress?" She'd paired a denim coat dress with a pair of boots. Though her hair was usually in a ponytail or braids, she'd left it down tonight. And hatless. She'd even added a few rare touches of makeup and the tiniest spritz of perfume. She knew she looked and smelled her best.

"I love your dress." He leaned in to give her a quick kiss on the cheek as he took his place beside her. "Most of all, I love the woman wearing it."

"Aw, thanks! You don't clean up too bad yourself, cowboy." She would never tire of seeing him in plaid shirts and jeans — not so long as she lived.

"I wish you'd quit dodging the question and tell me what's wrong."

"I'm just a little tired tonight." She faked a yawn. "It's been a long day."

"I've known you your entire life, Jules. Enough to

know the difference between when you're tired and when you're upset."

She maintained her silence, silently begging him to change the subject.

"My gut says you're still upset about your encounter earlier with a certain woman whose name shall not be named during our date this evening."

Then why bring her up at all? Despite her effort to squash it, Julia's anger sparked all over again. "You weren't exactly defending my mother when I walked over to the cash register."

"It wouldn't have done a bit of good, and you know it."

"You and Emerson were smiling and chatting up a storm with the person whose name shall not be named," Julia noted bitterly.

"Emerson was only tag-teaming the register to keep her away from me. That's why he left the bakery unmanned," he pointed out.

Though she knew he was telling the truth, she was having a hard time seeing past her own jealousy. The fact remained that he'd gone on a date with Rosie and shared a kiss with her. Every time Julia thought about it, it stung.

"Why did you ask her out in the first place?" she stormed, clasping her hands tightly in her lap.

He gripped the steering wheel, taking his time to answer. "I'm not sure the truth will make you feel any better."

"Try me," she snapped.

"Okay. I was trying to forget you. In case you're wondering, it didn't work."

She spoke through trembling lips. "I think she blames me for the fact that it didn't work out between the two of you."

"I have no control over what she thinks, Jules. All I can do is regret ever asking her out."

Though his words made her feel a little better, they didn't make the situation go away. "It's going to continue being a problem for her and me, I'm afraid." She bit her lower lip, hating how petty and jealous the admission made her sound.

"Why's that?"

"Because I honestly believe she still has hope in your direction," she exploded. "The kiss you shared with her must have been epic."

"I felt nothing," he growled. "What's it going to take to make you believe that?"

"I don't know," she cried piteously. "Time, maybe?" She hated knowing their conversation was ruining their date before they ever left the driveway.

He nodded grimly. "Fortunately, that's something we have plenty of, Jules."

"Can we just get on with our date?" she begged.

"Sure, we could go through the motions, but I love you too much to pretend like you're not angry with me." He drew a heavy breath. "And hurt."

"I'll get over it," she murmured tearfully. He was right. As miserable as she was right now, talking things out was better than pretending that everything was okay when it wasn't.

"Come here." He slid an arm behind her on the seat and used it to tug her closer.

She tipped her head against his shoulder, feeling emotionally wiped out.

"I was kind of hoping for a hug," he confessed quietly.

She wrapped her arms around his middle and allowed him to cuddle her closer.

"That's better." He enveloped her in a bear hug and sat there, simply holding her.

It felt so good to be held by him again. Everything was better in his arms. She wanted him to keep on holding her forever.

"So, ah." He abruptly tightened his arms around her. "I may have a solution to our current dilemma. Not sure you're going to like it, though, which is why I put you in a human straight-jacket first."

A chuckle escaped her at his less-than-illustrious description of the best hug she'd ever received. "What do you have in mind?"

"It's a pretty simple solution when you think about it. We need to quit keeping our relationship a secret."

She jolted at the reminder that it had been her idea to keep it quiet. Her intention had been to enjoy their rekindled romance in peace while they continued to find their way back to each other. She'd certainly not meant to string Rosie along in the process. It sort of killed her to realize she'd unintentionally done exactly that.

"If I admit you're right, how long are you going to gloat?" she grumbled into his shoulder.

A laugh shook his chest. "You have no idea how happy you just made me, do you?"

"Wow! You didn't even hesitate," she teased. "Let the gloating begin."

"Jules," he groaned, turning his head to brush his lips against her temple. "If you're paying me back for my crack about the straight-jacket…"

"Just give me one more night, okay, Dev?" She tipped her head back to gaze up at him. "Then we'll go public in the morning. You can post it all over social media, rent a billboard, or shout it from every rooftop on Cassidy Farm."

"Guess I better cancel our dinner reservation in town, huh?"

"That's fine with me."

"What would you like to do for dinner?"

"We could go for a walk or something. Pack a picnic, maybe." So long as they were alone, she didn't care.

"Done." He turned to face the steering wheel, still keeping one arm slung around her.

They were soon rolling toward Cassidy Farm, of all places. However, he didn't drive her toward the horse barns, or even toward the cabin he currently shared with his twin. Instead, he branched off on a gravel road on the left side of the property, driving her slowly between two vast pastures.

Cows grazed on both sides of them on fields dotted with large rolls of freshly cut hay. Though

Julia had seen quite a bit of Cassidy Farm while growing up, she didn't recall the gravel road they were on extending this far.

"Any chance you'll tell me where we're going?" she inquired shyly.

"Yep. My parents deeded off some land to each of us boys a while back. It dawned on me a few minutes ago that you've never seen my land."

"Oh, how generous of them, Dev!"

"It's not a hundred-and-twenty-four acres, mind you." He waggled his eyebrows playfully at her. "It's twenty."

It was still a lot. "Twenty acres times six boys is a hundred-and-twenty acres," she pointed out.

"Believe me, I'm grateful for every square inch of it." He eased off the gravel road and pulled directly into an empty field. They bumped their way across tufts of grass. As they headed toward the distant canyons, they were enveloped by shades of pink and purple light from the evening sun. It was like driving straight into the sunset.

He circled his truck around and brought it to a halt on a rose-drenched knoll. "This," he pointed out the window, "is where I'd like to build a house someday."

Her gaze followed where he pointed. Once again, they were facing toward Cassidy Farm, while the sun continued its descent on the horizon behind them. There were breathtaking views all around them.

"It looks like the perfect spot to me," she mused

contentedly. It was an entirely peaceful scene, parked there in the middle of the wide open countryside.

"Any chance my girl would be willing to browse house plans with me sometime soon?"

She was caught off guard by the question. "How soon?"

"As soon as possible. I'm twenty-six-years-old, Jules. I can't live with my brother forever."

"I, ah...sure!" Her heart raced at the thought of looking at house plans with him. It was a huge step, a serious step, and it touched her deeply that he wanted her to be a part of it.

"Thanks." He settled back against the seat cushion. "I say we watch the sunset together, then head back to the cabin to raid the fridge. Not sure if there's enough stuff at our bachelor pad to scrounge up a whole picnic, but we can try."

"The sunset is behind us," she reminded with a giggle. "If that's your way of saying you want to neck until it gets dark..."

"It is." He dipped his head over hers and paused right before his mouth touched hers. "If you'd rather do something else, though..."

She slid an arm around his neck and pulled his mouth the rest of the way down to hers.

CHAPTER 9: GROUND BREAKING

JULIA

Two days later

Julia paced the gravel driveway excitedly as she watched the construction crew from Amarillo caravan their way across her raw land. The air was filled with the roar of motors as they drove the mowers and grading equipment down their metal ramps and went to work.

Dust rose from all the scraping and smoothing. A breeze whistled from the distant canyons, picked it up, and dispersed it into a light brown haze. Julia could taste the grit in her mouth, which inevitably brought back memories from her rodeo days.

For a split second, her plan to build a racetrack faded. The vision was replaced by a long oval track filled with horses. Jockeys were bent over their necks, becoming one with the creatures as they urged them to continue running.

Oh. My. Lands.

Julia reached up to lower her sunglasses and blink over the top of them. Her uncle had gifted her with plenty of land. There was no reason she couldn't build some off-roading trails to have fun with and maybe even hold an official race now and then. However, what made so much more sense for her — as a barrel racing champ and the daughter of a quarter horse breeder — was to build a horse racing track. She couldn't believe it hadn't occurred to her before now.

Between her father's horse ranch, the county rodeo grounds, and Cassidy Farm serving as a thriving tourist trap, her race park would fit like the missing piece to their puzzle.

Snapping her sunglasses back into place, Julia hurried across the scrappy stretch of grass to flag down the project manager. She found her father chatting amicably with him in the shade of the tall metal garage.

They both looked up curiously as she strode their way.

"Change of plans," she announced brightly.

The two men listened intently to what she had to say. Grins split their faces as she described what she wanted.

Her father's friend scratched his bristled chin as he studied his work crew. "We were prepared to clear and grade all week." Lowering his hand, he continued, "However, I think we should stop and give you time to get back to the drawing board. Unless..." He and her father exchanged a knowing glance.

Her father spread his hands innocently. "No, I did not put her up to this."

Julia's head spun between the two men in puzzlement. "What aren't you guys telling me?"

Her father's friend shook his head. "I'm staying out of it."

"Dad?" she quizzed.

"Fine. The reason he's acting all quirky is because he happens to know I already paid to have a set of horse racing plans drawn up. The track, the grandstand, all of it."

"Oh, wow!" That wasn't something a person just did for no good reason. It took careful planning — many months of it — plus a decent chunk of change to draw up a set of plans like that. It could only mean one thing. Her father had been considering building a racetrack of his own for quite some time. "Why am I just now hearing about this?"

He shrugged. "Because Tonna got sick with cancer, and…" He shook his head. "It got pushed to the back burner, I guess."

"You want to build a racetrack," she repeated carefully. "You?"

"I breed and train quarter horses," he reminded. "It's not that big of a leap."

"So, what are you saying?" She propped her hands on her hips and faced him. There were at least a dozen other questions swimming through her head. "If you want me to stop, I will."

"Absolutely not!" He glared indignantly at her. "I

never really had time for a project like this. It never got past the point of a pipe dream."

"Baloney!" She stuck her chin out at him. "You paid for architectural drawings and everything."

"That I placed on the back burner. Permanently."

She cocked her head at him. "Why are you telling me this?"

"Because you're welcome to the plans if you want them. It'll save you thousands of dollars and months of time." He waved at his friend. "His company already has a copy on file. It means you could keep these tractors moving forward. It means—"

She launched herself into his embrace with a joyous whoop. "Thanks, Dad!"

"No problem, kid." He hugged her tightly.

"I hope this means you'll be staying on as my general contractor."

"I like the sound of that." He gave her ponytail a tug as he let her go.

"Only because I called you a general. I almost said senior advisor, but I knew you'd complain about it making you sound old."

"You're such a brat." He shook his head at his friend. "See what I have to put up with?"

His friend held up his hands. "Far be it from me to complain about your boss in front of your boss."

"Oh, I like him!" Julia nudged her father with her shoulder.

He slung an arm around her shoulders. "So long as you love me more, you got yourself a deal, kid."

"You're my absolute favorite dad in the whole wide world," she bragged with a giggle.

"Yep. You're a brat." He hugged her again.

"One hundred percent your brat," she reminded.

For an answer, he turned his head and pressed his lips to her temple.

———

Sunday

Cody felt a little ridiculous putting on a suit. It was kind of depressing, actually. He hadn't worn one in over two years — not since Tonna's memorial ceremony. He left his shirt and blazer off and shaved in his undershirt. His sense of discontentment grew. By the time he was patting on his aftershave, he felt like he was suffocating.

With a groan of irritation, he picked up his phone and mashed the speed dial button for Brooke.

She picked up on the second ring. "No, you are not getting out of going to church with me, Cody Benson. You promised!"

He gritted his teeth. "Do I really have to wear a suit?"

"No." She sounded surprised. "Jeans are fine."

"Good. Because I look like I'm headed to a funeral."

"You're actually in a suit?" Her voice rose to an incredulous squeak.

"I thought that's what folks wore to church." He

felt a little foolish at the realization that the only times he'd gone to church as an adult was to attend weddings and funerals.

"I bet you look amazing," she said softly.

"I can't breathe in this thing," he grumbled, though her words made him feel a little less like he was suffocating. Maybe it was just the after-effects of pneumonia.

"Then take it off."

He grimaced, suddenly wishing he could see her expression when she saw him in his suit. "How bad do you want to see me in it?"

"That's not a fair question."

"Why not?"

"Because I've never seen you in a suit, so of course I'm going for the suit if you give me a choice."

Right. It was a depressing reminder that she wasn't the bride who'd walked down the aisle to meet him at the altar over a decade ago. "Fine. I'll keep it on," he grumbled. "Just this once."

She chuckled. "Maybe a compromise is in order."

"Listening." He stomped from the bathroom to his closet to fish around for a pair of dress shoes.

"Leave off the tie and put on your boots and Stetson. I suspect your breathing will go back to normal."

He liked her suggestions so much that he immediately started making the changes. "You're right." He stood in front of the dressing mirror as he buttoned his shirt. "Looks like I'm still alive and breathing."

"Glad I could help you dress." She gave a tinkling laugh that warmed his insides.

"What are you wearing?" It suddenly dawned on him that he'd hardly ever seen her in anything but jeans.

"You'll find out when you pick me up." She chuckled again and disconnected the line.

Though he was dying to find out, he took a short detour to the convenience store on his way to the campground. He bought her a single red rose.

It was in his hand when he knocked on the door of her trailer.

When she appeared in the doorway, a filmy red dress was swirling around her knees. It had long sleeves and a V-neck. Like him, she was wearing her boots. She'd left off her Stetson, though. Her blonde hair hung in thick waves over her shoulders. She was so beautiful that he couldn't stop staring.

"Oh, how sweet of you, Cody!" Her delight in the single rose he handed her was so enormous that he inwardly kicked himself for not doing it sooner.

It matched the color of the dress she was wearing perfectly. It came pretty darn close to matching the blush wafting across her high cheekbones, as well.

She motioned for him to join her inside the trailer. "Don't need you hanging on to your hat and getting all scalded by the wind while I find something to put this in."

She opened and closed a few overhead cabinets and finally selected a tall clear glass to fill with water. Plopping the rose stem in it, she set the glass on the windowsill above her tiny sink. She stood there, beaming at it.

"It looks beautiful, doesn't it?"

"Very, very beautiful." Unable to resist the allure of Brooke's happy smile a second longer, Cody wedged himself between her and the sink and took her in his arms.

"Thank you." She stepped eagerly into his embrace.

She felt so good in his arms. So fragile, yet so strong. Someone who'd faced her demons and beat them. Someone who was trying with everything in her to turn over a new leaf.

She smelled amazing, too, like vanilla and honey. He suspected she'd been shopping at Cassidy Farm like most of the other women in town.

Everything about her enchanted him, right down to the strand of her hair that was clinging to his neck. It felt so intimate. So right.

Though he was in no hurry to let her go, he sensed she still wasn't ready to take things further between them. He decided to stretch out the moment by opening a topic he'd been wanting to run past her for days.

"I know we haven't had a chance to discuss it yet, but what do you think of Julia's switch to building a racetrack for horses?"

"I approve." Her head came off his shoulder, her blue gaze glowing with excitement. "I can tell you do, too."

"Ha!" It was so much more than that. "The kid is

living one of my biggest dreams."

"In that case," her smile was cautious, "I hope you don't mind that I've been reaching out to some of my contacts to help spread the word. A few celebrity endorsements would go a long way to getting our daughter established on the racing circuit."

She was right, and she knew it. The fact that she'd been working so hard to help out behind the scenes made his heart sing. Most of all, though, he reveled in the bond they shared through Julia. It had proven to be unbreakable.

"We should get going to church." He reluctantly dropped his arms and took a step toward the door.

"You don't approve of my interference in her life, huh?"

"What?" His head swiveled back in Brooke's direction.

"I'm sorry I didn't say something to you first. I should've asked before butting in."

He stomped back to her, reaching out to clasp her arms. "Brooke, you're amazing. Everything you're doing to help Julia is amazing. No, you don't need my permission to do stuff for our daughter. Now, let's go." He angled his head toward the door.

"Then why are you mad at me?" she cried.

"I'm not mad," he growled, looking pointedly at the door again. "What I'm trying to do is not kiss you. But you look so blasted beautiful in that blasted dress, on top of being the most blasted wonderful person I've ever met—"

She stretched to her tiptoes to brush her lips against his.

The sweetness of her gesture slammed into him, nearly rocking him off his feet. "Brooke," he cried against the edge of her mouth.

"I love you, Cody Benson," she sighed. "Even though I don't deserve you and probably never will."

"Love isn't something you earn," he growled, dragging his mouth over hers again. "It just happens."

"I don't want things to just happen between us," she protested softly. "I want to do things right this time around. I want to be your friend. To date. To really get to know you."

At the mention of the word *friend*, he stiffened. "I'm fine with dating, but don't you dare try to friend zone me, Brooke Flanagan. We're already more than friends. You know that."

She nodded, her gaze luminous with promise as he backed her toward the door.

"You never told me what you think of me in my suit," he reminded huskily as they strolled hand in hand to his truck.

A breathy giggle slid out of her. "Why do you think I kissed you?"

As hard as it was for him to go slow with her, he was thoroughly enjoying the flirting, the burn of attraction, the chase.

Even though the chase was taking him to church this morning. The directions Brooke gave him took them to a modern looking building — a metal warehouse type structure. Glass entrance doors opened to a brightly lit lounge and coffee shop. Three more sets of double doors led them to the sanctuary. It was painted mostly black. Upbeat bluegrass music was blaring through the surround sound speakers, and scenes of church and family were flashing across two big screens at the front of the room.

"It's a new building," Brooke murmured against his shoulder.

He eyed the laser lights and billowing smoke. "It feels like we just stepped into a concert hall."

"I know. Isn't it great?" She snuggled closer to him.

"I'm keeping an open mind." He'd been expecting something much quieter and less exciting. He should've known better. Brooke didn't do quiet. She'd always liked her music loud enough to feel the bass.

The Cassidy clan took up two entire rows on the left side of the building. He caught a glimpse of Julia standing by Devlin Cassidy's side, sandwiched between him and his twin.

Cody led Brooke down the aisle past them, searching for two empty seats together. He located them in the front row, no less. *That figures.*

Julia glanced up and caught his eye as they passed by her row. Her hands came up in a flutter of pure amazement.

He merely winked in return. No doubt their presence in the sanctuary had tongues wagging behind hands all across the room. That was one of the benefits of being in the front row, though. He and Brooke wouldn't have to witness any of it.

The minister was a young, skinny guy in sneakers, practically bouncing with energy. His button-up shirt was nicely pressed, but it wasn't even tucked in to his jeans.

Cody felt like he'd been defrauded. "Really?" he muttered in Brooke's ear as they took their seats. "You could've at least warned me how overdressed I was going to be."

"And miss seeing you in a suit?" She sent him a beauteous smile. "No way!"

Though he stuck out his tongue at her, it was impossible to work up any real anger. The navy suit had earned him a kiss, after all. Two of them, actually.

He forgot all about what he was wearing the moment the worship team took the stage. Everyone in the sanctuary stood for that portion of the service, and Cody got to be surprised all over again when he recognized one of the songs. He figured he must have heard it on the radio.

At first, he enjoyed simply being at Brooke's side. Soon, however, the words of the song started tugging at his heart. It was a message he'd never heard before, one about praying for protection over his family.

It spoke to his deepest, darkest fears. Never before had he felt so helpless to protect those he loved. No matter how much Brooke still blamed herself for her past mistakes, he was the one who'd failed to keep his family together. *Shoot!* He'd failed to even notice her addiction to alcohol. He'd also failed to see his parents' well-meaning but disastrous interference in their relationship. Then he'd married a woman who'd driven his daughter away from him, as well.

The way Cody saw it, he'd botched up just about everything he'd ever touched, and the last thing he wanted to do was botch it all up again.

As the song continued, something more powerful than he'd ever felt before nudged him forward. Hardly knowing what he was doing, he took a step toward the altar at the base of the stage, then another one. Since he and Brooke had been standing in the front row, it wasn't that far of a trip.

He stood before the altar, unsure of what to do next. All he knew was that he wanted the protection that they were singing about. There was nothing he wouldn't do, no price he wouldn't pay to get it.

"Please, God." The words burst from deep within him. "Show me how to protect my family." He couldn't lose Brooke and Julia again. He just couldn't.

Hands descended on his shoulders. Lots of hands. He heard the low murmur of men's voices, as friends and neighbors began to pray with him. Then the minister appeared in front of him and asked to lead him in a prayer of salvation.

"Sure." He had no interest in leaving the building as the same cranky, middle-aged man who'd walked in. If there was more to be had in life, he wanted it — all of it.

More friends and neighbors joined them at the altar as they prayed together. Ridge Cassidy was among them. Though Ridge was only a few years older than Cody, he walked with a limp from an injury sustained during his rodeo days. His oldest son, Asher, was at his side, looking like a younger, more scarred version of his father, thanks to a freak barn fire a few years back. Both leaned in at some point or another to shake his hand and clap him on the back, acting like he'd just made the best decision of his life.

When he finally turned around to walk back to his seat, he was surprised to discover most of the church was praying. A lot of folks were hugging the person standing next to them. Others were turned around, praying for someone standing in the row behind them. A young, brown-haired woman he'd never seen before had her hands resting on Brooke's shoulders, speaking earnestly to her.

Brooke was nodding in return, blinking back tears.

The woman smiled at Cody as he approached them. "I'm Francine." She held out a hand. "The pastor's wife."

He clasped her hand. "Pleased to meet you."

She gave a damp-sounding chuckle. "I think you just started a revival, Mr. Benson."

"Me?" He touched his chest.

"Yes, you. All it takes is one spark to light a fire."

She waved a hand to take in the entire room. "After you walked down to the altar, this broke out. Isn't it wonderful?"

He wasn't sure what to make of it. He was simply grateful to no longer be the center of everyone's attention. "Honestly? I was just praying for protection over my family."

She nodded, smiling warmly. "Something tells me you're going to get everything you asked for, Mr. Benson."

"I sure hope so, ma'am." He returned to Brooke's side and slid an arm around her waist. "If it happens, all the credit goes to her for insisting I come to church this morning."

"It's already happening," Francine assured. "You'll see."

"I like her," Brooke confided as she and Cody walked up the aisle and exited the church together.

"Me, too."

A feminine squeal from behind them made them halt before they reached his truck. It was Julia.

She sailed across the parking lot in their direction. Dev Cassidy followed behind her at a slower pace, grinning like an idiot. Like her mother, Julia was wearing a dress. Not red, though. Hers was a blue and white striped t-shirt dress tied at the waist. She'd paired it with a sassy pair of high-heeled cowgirl boots.

Man! If going to church meant Cody was going to get to see his two favorite women in dresses more often, he'd never miss another service.

"Y'all sure know how to make an entrance," his daughter chuckled. "I about lost it when I saw you walk down the aisle. It was seriously the last thing on this planet I ever expected to see."

"Gee, thanks!" Cody rolled his eyes at his daughter. "Didn't realize you viewed me as a complete heathen."

"Hey! You said it, not me." She stepped closer to give him and her mom a hug.

"Since when did *you* start going to church?" He narrowed his gaze suspiciously on hers.

"Since a few years ago, you heathen," she retorted.

"Not anymore," he reminded, grinning.

"I'm so glad." She hugged him again and stepped back.

Devlin Cassidy, who'd been standing at the edge of their huddle, reached for her hand.

Cody caught his gaze and held it for a long, assessing moment. Then he gave the cowboy a slow nod. They needed to talk about his intentions toward Julia soon. When Devlin nodded back, Cody knew he understood. He'd text him to set up a time and place for them to meet, maybe over coffee.

"Hey, sir." The young cowboy inclined his head respectfully at Cody. "My parents asked if I'd extend an invitation for y'all to join us at Cassidy Farm today for lunch." His smile included Brooke.

When Cody hesitated, she jumped in. "We'd love to," she gushed, laying a hand on Cody's arm.

He was a little disappointed, since he'd been

looking forward to taking her out to lunch, just the two of them. However, the warning pressure on his forearm told him that she very much wanted to accept the Cassidys' kind invitation. It was beginning to look as if he was going to be stuck in his suit all afternoon. *Bummer!*

Devlin looked relieved. "You can follow us if you want."

"I know the way." Cody watched him lead Julia to a black pickup truck a few parking spots down from where he was parked. "Guess we'll be sharing her with him from now on," he growled, trying to decide if he liked the idea. He'd just gotten her back. In some ways, it was like losing her all over again.

"He'll keep her in town," Brooke noted brightly.

"I reckon." There was that. He shot her a grateful look. "You always know what to say."

"It's true, Cody. The Cassidys' roots run deep in Chipper. The boys' grandfather settled this town. They're here to stay."

He nodded as he lifted her into his truck. "What about you, Brooke? You said you weren't ready to leave yet. Does that mean you're here to stay, too?"

Her smile slipped. "It depends."

"On what?"

"Whether you want me to stay."

"Of course, I want you to stay." He couldn't believe she had to ask. "Not in that blasted trailer, though. I want you to come home. To be my wife and the mother of our daughter for as long as we have left together."

"Oh, Cody!" She pressed both hands to her heart. "What if I fall off the wagon?"

"Then we'll deal with it together, same as any other couple." He frowned thoughtfully at her. "How long have you been sober?" He couldn't believe he'd not gotten around to asking her yet.

"Five years."

His eyes widened. It was an incredible accomplishment. She was well on her way to recovery. "What kept you sober so long?"

She smiled faintly. "Mostly my faith. Once I started going to church, I realized I no longer had to do it alone. I have help." She pointed upward.

"And now you have me."

She caught her breath, looking so hopeful that he reached for her hand.

"Do you want to know why I walked down to the altar to pray for protection this morning?"

She nodded mutely.

"Because it's something I failed to do on my own. Something I'm apparently not strong enough to do on my own." He raised her hand to his lips. "I'm confident my prayer was heard. So confident that if we weren't sitting in my truck right now, I'd be on a knee in front of you. Probably on both knees, telling you how much I still love you." He kissed her fingers. "Brooke, I asked you something many years ago, and I'm about to ask you again. That's the other thing I prayed about this morning — that you would give me a different answer this time."

"Yes, Cody." Her voice was trembly with

emotion. "My answer is yes."

He almost couldn't believe his ears. "Thank you, Brooke." He looked forward to spending the rest of his life proving she'd finally given him the right answer. "I want to kiss you, but I'm not sure that necking in a church parking lot is my thing."

She chuckled. "It's not my thing, either."

Instead of driving straight to Cassidy Farm, he made a quick detour home.

Brooke shook her head at him. "You just had to get out of that suit, huh?"

"Nah. Since you like it so much, I think I can suffer in it a little longer." He leaned over to run a finger down her cheek. "Sit tight. I'll be right back."

He returned a few minutes later with the black velvet box he'd kept locked in his safe for two and a half decades. Only after he was seated beside her in the truck again did he flip open the lid.

"Cody!" She stared at the small white round solitaire. "It's so beautiful!" She held out her hand so he could slide the ring on.

He was pleased that it still fit. "I can buy you a lot bigger one now, Brooke."

"I want this one, please." Her heart was in her eyes as she beheld the lovely gemstone.

"I love you, Brooke. I always will." He angled her chin just right so he could settle his mouth over hers, tender and cherishing. Like the ring, their lips were still a perfect fit.

"I love you, too," she whispered.

He deepened the kiss.

CHAPTER 10: QUICK TRIGGER
DEVLIN

Six months later

Dev eased his horse trailer onto the newly paved road leading to Julia's horse racing track. He nodded a welcome to the members of the masonry team, who looked up and waved when he drove past. They were building a wide, stacked stone sign. When it was completed, gold letters would be mounted to it to spell out Twin Canyons Park. Julia's decision to name her racetrack after the canyon views she'd grown up with had gotten a big thumbs up by the townsfolk.

The original gravel driveway had been widened to a quadruple set of lanes, accented by brightly painted orange and white stripes — two running into the park and two running out of the park. There were wide shoulders on each side, providing ample pull-off space. Despite the small size of Chipper, Julia remained forward thinking in her expectation that the races would draw large, out-of-town crowds. She was positioning her business for success.

The grading and packing of the track soil layers was complete, as well. All in all, it had been an extensive process. To an onlooker, it might simply appear to be a dirt track. However, it was so much more than that. Julia had insisted on the finest craftsmanship to provide the maximum comfort for the horses that would be running on it. Her construction crew had built it on a six-inch cement base for stabilization, followed by six inches of limestone, topped by a double layer of sandy loam. The center of the track and guest areas of the park had been sodded with a thick Bermuda cushion. A triple water feature graced the center of the track, three small lakes accented by water spouts for aeration.

Her construction crew was present this morning and hard at work on the finishing touches. They were erecting quarter mile markers and mounting the newly engraved swing doors on the gate stalls. It was a massive starting line gate with no less than twelve stalls.

It had certainly given the locals something new to gossip about. Their excitement over the past several months as they watched the new track take shape had done nothing but escalate. If anything, it was reaching a razor-sharp edge of anticipation as the day of the opening races approached. The many visits Chipper had already received so far from rodeo and racing legends alike were the talk of the town.

The city officials could thank Brooke Flanagan for

that. Endorsements were quite literally rolling in, thanks to her constant stream of invitations to her celebrity friends. The Twin Canyons Park grand opening would take place in less than a month, and it was shaping up to be a very well attended event.

Every hotel in the vicinity was already booked to capacity. Even the campgrounds were fully rented out. Airbnb rooms were popping up all over the county as families raced against time to renovate outbuildings, barn lofts, and unoccupied recreational vehicles.

Dev feathered his brakes and nosed into one of the truck and trailer spots in a side parking lot built especially for competitors. Since his window was rolled down, he could hear the whirr of drills and the ping of hammers. The last of the aluminum race rails were being set in place. Julia had chosen goose neck posts to allow for more room for future grading and maintenance.

He leaped down from the truck cab and opened the horse trailer, quickly saddling Quick Trigger. Though the palomino's feisty temperament hadn't changed much, he'd come a long way in terms of training — far enough to be saddled and ridden around a track. Dev hoped to have him ready to race during the upcoming season.

Julia met them at the starting gate. "You made it, babe!" Though she beamed a happy smile at him, she walked up to Quick Trigger first.

"You are most definitely the star of this morning's

show, buddy. Are you ready to test out my racetrack?"

Quick Trigger tossed his white mane and nickered a response, butting his nose against her gloved hand.

"Huh-uh, you greedy beast!" She affectionately brushed her fingers up and down his nose to soften her words. "You know how it goes. Work comes first. The rewards come later."

Dev had never seen anything more beautiful than the sight of his favorite horse nuzzling his favorite woman.

Julia was in an unbuttoned pink and white plaid shirt this morning with the sleeves rolled up at the elbows, a sassy white tank top that hugged her beautiful curves, and a pair of comfortable jeans that were worn plumb through at the knees. Her hair was pulled back in two thick blonde braids that hung from beneath her straw Stetson.

Dev stepped up behind her and angled his head to nip a kiss at her cheek. It was no easy task, maneuvering around the brims of both their hats, but he managed. "Any chance you'll make an exception for your boyfriend on the reward side of things?" His voice was husky with adoration against her ear.

"Mmm. I don't know if that's wise." She melted against his chest for a moment. "Quick Trigger can get pretty impatient when he's kept waiting."

"Maybe you should've considered that before waking up so beautiful. Like my poor horse that you've bewitched, I can't resist you, Jules." His warm trail of kisses down the side of her neck made her shiver.

She didn't resist when he cuddled her closer. Her soft little laugh went straight to his heart. "I have no makeup on, Dev."

"So? You don't need it." He hooked an arm around her middle to anchor her more firmly against him.

"I'm also wearing my oldest pair of jeans."

"You're wearing them so well that I can't take my eyes off you, darling."

Another breathy chuckle escaped her. "Ooo, were you checking me out while I was working, Mr. Cassidy?"

"Always, Miss Benson."

"Careful." She continued stroking one finger down the horse's nose. "I think you're making Quick Trigger jealous."

"Don't care." He spun her around, pulled off her Stetson, and dipped her low over his arm. The kiss they shared made his chest pound and his breathing turn rough.

When he stood her up to set her hat back on her head, Quick Trigger leaned over and gave him a sharp nip on the shoulder.

"Ow!" Dev glared at him, though he wasn't really angry.

"I tried to warn you." Laughter warmed Julia's voice as she pressed a small handful of chopped up carrots into his hand. "You'd best make it up to him before you hit the racetrack together."

"You da boss," he teased, accepting the carrots and feeding them to his horse.

Quick Trigger nibbled them from his fingers a little harder than he needed to.

Dev playfully flicked his nose. "You're such a rabble-rouser."

Quick Trigger nickered again. Dev could've sworn the horse was laughing at him. "Did you hear that?" He waggled an accusing finger at the palomino and almost got bitten again.

"He's got attitude for sure." Julia smiled affectionately at the beast as she reached up to pat his neck. "I'm kind of dying to see what he can do on a full-sized track."

So was Dev. He moved to stand beside the horse. "You ready for the bright lights and sound of applause, boy?"

Quick Trigger pawed the ground once, but otherwise stood still while Dev mounted him and settled into the saddle.

Julia blew a kiss at him. "Take him to the first stall and wait until you hear me over the loudspeaker."

"Roger dodger, darling." Dev gave her a mock salute.

She rubbed her hands like a small child standing in front of a pile of Christmas gifts. Then she backed away from them to hop inside a grass green Gator utility vehicle bearing the new Twin Canyons Park logo on its hood. She drove it to the four-story glassed-in grandstand on the other side of the racetrack and disappeared inside the building.

The lower level offered concessions and a sit-down restaurant. The next level housed most of the administrative offices. The upper two levels consisted of penthouse suites. Over half were already booked for the opening day's festivities.

She had the water spouts in the center of the track turned on. Dev wasn't sure all of this was necessary for a test run, but his girlfriend had insisted on making Quick Trigger's test run as close to a real run as possible. Because of how strongly the breeze was whipping through the stadium, Dev could feel a light mist of over-spray drifting down on his face and hands.

His horse pranced a little in anticipation as they made their way to Gate One and took their position behind the door.

It was a gorgeous spring morning, not too hot and not too cold. Behind them was the cluster of horse barns. Six were complete. Four more were under construction. Julia had plans to build at least a dozen more after that, but she was waiting to justify the additional building projects until after she turned a profit on the place. Between races and racing seasons, she planned to offer up the facility for private party rentals.

There was some muttering and murmuring among the skeptics that the Benson girl was biting off more than she could chew. Every chance Dev got, though, he encouraged her to ignore the naysayers. It was a no-risk-no-reward kind of business. If she didn't go big, she might as well pack her toys and go home.

She had some pretty big sponsors, not the least of which was the Silver Streak. She also had her father advising her every step of the way. What the owner of the Silver B Ranch knew about horses was pure gold. So long as Julia kept her nose to the grindstone, Dev saw no reason why she couldn't turn her newest venture into a success.

Her voice rang out over the loudspeaker, reclaiming his attention. "I'd like to welcome Quick Trigger on his debut run to the not-yet-open-to-the-public Twin Canyons Park. His rider is none other than the cowboy who stole my heart, Devlin Cassidy — rancher and store manager from Cassidy Farm."

The recording of a cheering crowd filled the air. Dev grinned at her antics, imagining her pushing buttons on her new sound effects machine.

"For all of you working and listening in here at the park today, I'm asking that you hold your drills, hammers, tractors, and other equipment silent. For the next fifteen minutes, we'll be conducting our first full-stadium test run. Thank you for your cooperation, and thank you for being a part of making Chipper's first racetrack a reality. We will make another announce-ment to let you know when this test is concluded."

The television screens and score charts flashed to life, and music played in the interim. Julia ran through a few more announcements, then gave the signal to start the race.

Gate One swung open in front of Dev. He dug in his heels, and Quick Trigger took off at a sprint. His horse loved to run, the faster the better. He quickly accelerated to a full gallop, pounding his way across the professionally packed dirt track.

Though Dev was sitting in a forward position over the horse's neck, never taking his eyes off the track, he was aware of construction workers and members of the skeleton stadium crew moving closer to the rails. A few men shouted encouragement. Quick Trigger actually increased his speed in response.

This is good. Dev was no professional jockey and wouldn't be the one riding in the actual races on opening day. However, he sensed that the horse moving beneath him was thriving on the energy and excitement around them. It made Dev irritated all over again that the horse's first owner had claimed he was anything less than racing material. Quick Trigger was acting like he was born for this.

A glint of sunlight on silver alerted him to the fact that there was an impediment in his lane. As he rounded the curve, he discovered that one of the sections of aluminum railing had been left on the track. Though there wasn't much time, he slowed Quick Trigger's speed and swung him wide through the curve.

As they reached the outside of the track, a section of the railing on that side came loose and started to tumble to the dirt.

What the—? Dev watched in horror, knowing

there wasn't enough time to adjust his course again. For a moment, the whole world seemed to slow as Quick Trigger's hooves churned through the dirt.

Dev's mind raced over his options during the split second he had left to deliberate, and he could only come up with one. He was going to have to jump the horse over the fallen rail. Though Quick Trigger's first owner had wanted him trained as a jumper for his teenage daughter to compete with, jumping wasn't something Dev had ever practiced with the horse. He'd avoided it on purpose after hearing about what a bad experience Quick Trigger had endured with his previous owner.

Time to find out if you remember any of it, boy. Dev's last thought as he raised himself slightly out of the saddle was that he wished he'd taken the leap and proposed to Julia already. If he and Quick Trigger didn't make it through the jump, one or both of them could be severely injured or worse.

He balanced forward in a bent position, pushed his weight into his heels, and held his hands forward. Never taking his eyes from the track, he held his breath as Quick Trigger tensed beneath him. In the next moment, they sailed over the fallen rail.

Dev reined the horse in as quickly as he could afterward. It took several strides for Quick Trigger to slow his speed. He came to a shuddering halt, breathing hard from his efforts.

"You did good, boy!" Dev patted his neck. "Real good!" He glanced behind him at the debris on the track, wondering how in the world they'd suffered two fallen rails during the same test run. It didn't feel like an accident.

Out of the corner of his eye, he saw a man running away from the track, bent nearly double.

Dev shouted at him to stop.

All he did was give one quick glance back. His dark gaze glinted with malice from the two eye holes in his mask.

"Stop that man!" Dev pointed at the retreating figure, and a pair of construction workers took up the chase. The man in the mask was tackled to the ground in a matter of seconds.

Dev rode Quick Trigger in their direction. He could hear the rumble of a Gator motor behind him and figured Julia was on her way, as well. He hoped she'd already called the police.

This was sabotage. No way around it. A deliberate attempt to harm a horse and his rider. But why? It made no sense. Sure, the citizens of Chipper liked to gossip, but that was about the extent of their meanness. Nothing like this had ever happened in their town.

He leaped down from Quick Trigger. The saboteur was trying to wrestle free from those holding him down, but he gave up when a third construction worker added his strength to the mix.

Julia parked her Gator and jogged over to the quickly growing crowd of onlookers. "Everyone, remain calm, please. The police are on their way."

Sirens sounded in the distance. It was such a quick response to her call that Dev figured they must have already been in the area. *Lucky us!* He'd never before been so grateful to see a white cruiser drive into view.

Instead of a single trooper, a pair of troopers climbed from the car. Julia rushed to explain what had happened. Then she led them to the man her workers had detained.

One of the troopers leaned over to snatch the black mask off the saboteur's head.

Rosie McKeever's younger brother stared defiantly back. A murmur of amazement rose. It was clear that several of those gathered recognized who he was.

"Why?" Julia's amazed question tore at Dev's heart, because he already knew why.

"Because you messed with my sister's feelings!" He pointed in accusation at Dev. "She loved you, but you dropped her like a hot potato the moment your snobby ex marched back into town and crooked her little finger at you."

His foolish confession had him in handcuffs in short order. He was still shouting insults when the police led him away for booking.

Julia jogged over to Dev. "Are you okay?" Her voice shook as she ran her hands lightly over his shoulders and chest, probing for injuries.

"I'm fine, and Quick Trigger is fine."

"I'm so thankful!" A shudder worked its way through her as she produced a bag of treats and proceeded to slather Quick Trigger with apple slices, carrot bits, and attention.

Her voice hitched as she murmured soft words of praise to him. "You are the most amazing horse, Quick Trigger. I didn't even know you knew how to jump." She glanced back at Dev, a thousand questions burning in her eyes.

"We haven't done any jumping together," he admitted, pointing upward. "I think Someone up there was clearly looking after us down here."

She gulped and nodded. "I don't know what I would've done if anything had happened to you, Dev." Mindless of those still milling around them, she waved her hands at the racetrack and quavered, "None of this would mean anything to me if you weren't here."

He knew the feeling. As they led Quick Trigger back to the horse trailer together, he tried to lighten her mood. "Everything is going to be okay, Jules."

"How can you say that?" Her voice rose indignantly. "You almost died out there this morning!"

"But I didn't."

"I'm just floored, Dev. I get that Rosie McKeever is disappointed and upset, but her brother took things way too far. Not only was he trying to harm you, he would've shut down my business before we had the chance to officially open."

"Yeah, well, he should have read his Bible more closely. The part that says no weapon formed against us shall prosper." Dev reached over to touch her cheek and steer her gaze back to him. "And it didn't."

She drew a shuddery breath, nodding. "I'm still

probably going to have nightmares for the rest of my life over this." She couldn't help wondering if what had happened out there was partly her fault. Her last encounter with Rosie hadn't exactly been a pleasant one.

"No, you won't." His voice was firm. "The Lord never promised us a cake walk, but He did promise He would never leave us or forsake us. He's with us, Jules. He'll always be with us, and we'll live to fight another day."

After he loaded his horse into the trailer, she moved to stand directly in front of her boyfriend. "In case I wasn't clear back there, I can't bear the thought of living without you, Dev. I don't want to. You're so right for me. I just wish it hadn't taken me so long to figure it out."

"I think you knew it from the start," he corrected, taking her into his arms. "I was right for you back then, and I'm right again for you now."

"Yes." Her expression was so dreamy that he couldn't tear his gaze away from her.

Man! He'd planned out the perfect evening. He'd gone so far as to write out the words to tell her everything that was on his heart, but now seemed liked the time to say them. No more waiting.

He dropped to a knee in front of her. "Jules, we've had so many false starts and mixed signals that I almost gave up hope. Fortunately, God saw fit to give us another chance, and I'm taking it. Will you marry me and make me the happiest man in the state of Texas?"

Waiting for her response was the most agonizing thing he'd ever endured. The first time he'd asked her to marry him, she'd been equally tongue-tied. He hoped it wasn't a bad sign that she wasn't immediately answering him this time around.

Looking like she'd been struck by lightning, she nodded at long last, tugging his hands and silently pleading with him to stand.

He rose and faced her, lacing both hands through hers. "Please tell me that's a yes."

"Yes, Dev." Her voice shook. "I'm all yours. I always have been."

He leaned in to accept her gift with the tenderest of kisses.

CHAPTER 11: OPENING DAY

JULIA

Opening day

Julia stood in the grandstand with her fiancé at her side, feeling a little self-conscious about the size of the diamond he'd put on her hand. It was, quite simply, the most enormous oval diamond she'd seen outside of a museum.

Dev's large hand was splayed warmly across her lower back, buoying her spirits in a way that nothing else could on a day like today. She loved that they'd finally made their engagement official. After what Rosie's brother had pulled, it seemed prudent to make their feelings known. The young saboteur was currently cooling his heels behind bars, though he was expected to make bail soon. Rosie had left town altogether, which was probably for the best.

Though Julia's stomach was full of butterflies from worrying about every detail about today, things had gone smoothly so far. To thank her mother for her love, support, endorsement, and investment in the racetrack, Julia had asked her to open the ceremonies.

Brooke Flanagan entered the grandstand and made her way to the microphone. "This is it," she announced brightly to those who were gathered. The diamond solitaire flashed from her finger, making Julia wonder all over again why her parents hadn't set a date yet for their wedding. What were they waiting for?

She caught her father's eye as he moved to stand behind her mother. He'd shaved and thrown a navy blazer over his white button-up shirt and jeans. He even had on silver cufflinks that she was pretty sure were a gift from her mother. She'd honestly never seen him dress up as often as he did now that he was dating Brooke Flanagan. For a middle-aged guy, he wasn't too shabby in the hotness department, either. Tanned, broad-shoulders, and a lopsided smile that the women his age seemed to seriously dig.

He winked at her before returning his gaze to her mother. She'd never seen him look this happy, so she decided on the spot that she was just going to have to stop worrying about their wedding date. She supposed they would tie the knot when they were good and ready. But why weren't they ready? She scowled again in her father's direction, but he didn't look her way again.

The sound tech guy flipped on Brooke Flanagan's microphone, and she started to speak. "Welcome to the first-ever Twin Canyons Park races!"

Her words were met with a deafening round of applause from the audience. The silver stands and bench seating areas were packed. The overflow of guests was crowded around the railings and milling in the grassy areas. Some had pitched blankets on the grassy slopes and were lounging there as well.

Brooke went on to thank the sponsors, endorsers, community leaders, construction crews, stadium employees, contestants, friends, families, and guests for making today possible. Then she got right to the heart of her presentation.

"Many of you know me as the Silver Streak." Her words were met with another thunderous round of applause. "What most of you probably don't know is that I've battled an addiction to alcohol for most of my career." The stands grew abruptly quiet. "Like so many rodeo riders, who buckle beneath the pressure of performing, I didn't feel like I could make it from one day to the next without constant trips to the liquor store. But all that changed the day I encountered the Circle of Hope." She went on to describe the faith-based group in more detail and how they'd helped her turn her life around. A significant percentage of today's proceeds would go toward their efforts to help other athletes like her. She gave out their hotline number for those in need of free counseling. "I am happy to report that, because of my encounter with the Circle of Hope, I've been sober for over five straight years."

Her listeners shot to their feet at her words and started clapping again.

It was a while before she could continue. "Because of this program, I got my life back, my family back, my home and my community back. I am living proof that second chances do exist. So, thank you, thank you, thank you from the bottom of my heart for supporting such a worthy cause at today's opening festivities." She paused and glanced over at Julia. "At this time, it is my greatest honor to hand the microphone over to the amazing owner of our all-new Twin Canyons Park and racetrack — my very own daughter and barrel-racing world champion, Julia Benson!"

Julia reached for Dev's hand and towed him with her to the podium as she delivered the final opening remarks. The first race started in a flurry of cheers and a blur of motion as horses and riders erupted from their gates.

———

Emerson watched his twin up in the bandstand from one of the benches below it. Though the Cassidys had reserved a private suite on the VIP balcony of the clubhouse, he wasn't in the mood to be immersed in so much love and happiness. Two of his sisters-in-law, Bella and Jade, were cuddling newborn babies. Cormac had an adopted son, and his new wife was pregnant. Their mom, Claire, was probably billing and cooing like a turtledove over her growing bevy of grandchildren, which she was starkly determined to have more of. She was constantly making him and

Fox feel guilty for remaining single. Fox acted like he didn't care, but Emerson did.

Yep. Everyone in his family was sickeningly happy besides him. He'd never imagined how alone he would feel if his twin brother found love before he did. They'd always had each other's backs and shared everything, but this was something Dev couldn't share.

To make matters worse, Emerson didn't have so much as a prospect on the horizon. That was the tough thing about living in a small town. The only woman who even remotely interested him was the current Miss Texas. Unfortunately, his brothers were completely right in their constant jokes about his crush on her. She was way out of his league.

A woman winning the hearts and minds across the state of Texas with her endless humanitarian causes did not need a small town cowboy turned store manager for a boyfriend. Not that he'd bothered asking her out. He had no interest in making that much of a fool of himself.

That didn't keep him from dreaming, though. He was surprised that she'd continued to text and call him after agreeing to his request to serve as master of ceremonies for the upcoming rodeo. Normally, he wouldn't have expected to hear from her again until a few days before the event. She probably didn't mean anything by it, but still.

He wished he could stop himself from reading too much into it, but he'd been on edge for days now — feeling like his life had boiled down to living from text to text. Unfortunately, it had been three days since their last texting frenzy, and the silence from her was driving him crazy. During that conversation, she'd asked all sorts of questions about today's races. It was the first time she'd even mentioned her interest in horse racing.

He'd shared all the information he could, and now crickets.

"Excuse me, please, ma'am. Pardon me, sir."

No way! The familiar female voice had his head jerking to the left. For a moment, he thought he was dreaming, but there she was.

Miss Texas herself. Lacey Perry in the flesh. And she was threading her way through his row in his direction.

Though her almond-shaped eyes were hidden behind an enormous pair of sunglasses, her long, curly black hair was a dead giveaway to her real identity. Most women on the planet didn't have hair as long as Lacey Perry. Or so many freckles sprinkled across her sun-kissed cheeks. Or a heart of such pure altruism. She was an incredible human being — one he'd been avidly following on social media and crushing on for the past two years.

"Hey, Emerson!" She fluttered a little wave at him as she slowly worked her way to his side.

"Hey!" He dared not say her name aloud, knowing she preferred her anonymity. Shooting a quick glance around them, he was amazed that the audience had not already erupted into the flash of a thousand phone camera bulbs and pleas for her autograph.

He waited until she was wedged in between him and the fellow on the other side of her before dipping his head to speak directly in her ear. "What are you doing here?" He didn't see so much as a single body-guard hovering. "Alone," he added tersely.

Her long white sundress was aflame with bright flowers. He couldn't believe she was drawing this much attention to herself. It fell nearly to her ankles, which were encased in metallic gold sandals. A bright pink rose was tucked into her hair behind one ear.

"I'm not alone." Her dark eyes sparkled teasingly at him from behind her sunglasses. "I'm with you."

At his stunned look, she quickly added, "Okay, I've got two bodyguards watching from a discreet distance, plus a camera man and my personal assistant."

His eyebrows rose even higher. "So this is some sort of publicity stunt?"

"Yes and no."

"What's that supposed to mean?"

"It means I'm here because I want to be, cowboy."

A commotion behind them caused someone to bump into her shoulder.

Without thinking, he steadied her by sliding an arm around her slender waist. Then, because it felt so good there, he left it.

She leaned closer to him, tipping her face up to his to regard him expectantly.

He had no idea what she wanted from him, but she didn't impress him as someone who did something for no reason at all. "You okay?"

"More than okay. My flight was smooth. No delays. I did have a little trouble hailing a cab here. It's a pretty busy day in Chipper."

He felt the air leave his lungs. "You did not just flag down a common cab!"

"Why not? Like I said, I brought my entourage with me." She smiled sunnily up at him, probably not realizing how tantalizingly closer it brought their mouths.

He was aware of it, though, painfully so. It was like his last hundred daydreams had decided to come to life all at the same time, which was completely unfair.

"I think of a dozen security reasons why it's not a good idea," he scolded. "Not even with your entourage."

"Are we still talking about Chipper, Texas?" She wrinkled her nose, looking perplexed. "Because I've seriously never felt safer in my life."

Yeah, he used to think the same thing about his hometown, but Chipper was growing, and times were changing. "You should've called me," he insisted. He would have dropped everything to go pick her up.

"I did. Can't believe you blew me off like that."

As he frantically dug his phone out of his pocket, she started laughing. "Gotcha!" she crowed. "I lied. I didn't call you, because I was actually hoping to surprise you."

"Well, you succeeded." He stuffed his phone back in his pocket, shaking his head at her.

"Good, because I didn't know what else to do for your birthday."

"My birthday!" He felt like an idiot, echoing her words like that, but he couldn't help it. "It's not for another week."

"I know, but I was able to move some things around on my schedule, which allowed me to take the whole week off. No way was I going to just barely miss the opening day of the Twin Canyons Park. This is huge, Emerson. It's seriously all over the news."

"That's, uh, great!" He wondered if he looked as dazed as he sounded. "So, are you here with that Circle of Hope group?" She seemed to have a finger in every charity.

"No. I really am here to personally deliver your birthday present."

"Are you serious?" He knew he was staring, but he couldn't help it. Couldn't seem to tear his gaze from her animated features.

She abruptly pulled away from him. "Omigosh! If I misread something in our emails, and you already have a girlfriend or—"

"No," he interrupted hastily. "I don't." For the life of him, he couldn't figure out what he'd typed in his emails that made her think he was interested in dating her. He was *very* interested, of course. He just wasn't sure how she'd figured it out from their emails, which he'd been careful to keep professional.

But if you're in the market for a boyfriend, darling, I am ALL yours!

"So, you *do* want me here?" She anxiously scanned his face.

He couldn't believe she felt the need to ask. "I want you here." He was still having trouble believing that she was, in fact, here, but he reckoned his brain would eventually catch up with that amazing fact.

"You don't seem too happy about it."

"Lacey!" He turned his head to speak against her temple. "I'm glad you're here. Someone should pinch me or punch me to make sure I'm not dreaming, though. Oomph!" He sucked in a breath as her slender fist made contact with his ribs.

"Little known fact," she murmured against his earlobe. "I'm a black belt. If you'd like me to hit you harder—"

"Nah! That's alright." He gave a pained chuckle, rubbing his ribcage. "I get the idea."

"I'm not sure that you do, cowboy." Her smile slipped. "Because you still haven't convinced me that you're glad I traveled all the way from Dallas to celebrate your birthday with you."

His heart pounded with awareness as she cupped one delicate hand around the back of his neck to tug his head down to hers.

Well, I'll be! He might not be a genius, but he was bright enough to catch on when a woman was angling for a kiss. He still had no earthly idea why

Lacey was angling for one from him, but he aimed to please.

Touching his mouth gently to hers, he savored the rush of wonder that inevitably came with any first kiss. But it was so much more than that. Her scent and vibrancy surrounded him. Her beauty enveloped him. The eagerness of her touch and the way her lips moved against his utterly entranced him.

"Why me, Lacey?" he muttered against her lips.

She tipped her head back against his shoulder to study him with luminous eyes through her sunglasses. "Did you think I wouldn't find out?"

He shook his head helplessly. "Lacey, you just kissed me silly. I'm not capable of playing guessing games right now." All he could think about was how much he wanted to kiss her again.

"I'm talking about all those boxes of honey lotion and shampoo you sent to the orphanage in Dallas. Is that ringing a bell?"

"Nope." He scowled down at her, wondering what she was talking about.

"Liar!" She drew a caressing finger down his cheek.

"Listen, if you're looking for a donation from Cassidy Farm, I'm sure I can arrange something."

"You're amazing, Emerson Cassidy. Truly amazing." As she stretched on her tiptoes to kiss him again, his mind raced over the possibilities. "I've never before met anyone less interested in receiving credit for everything you've done for the orphanage."

Everything I've done? If anyone had sent a donation from Cassidy Farm without his knowledge, he could think of only one likely culprit.

Fox.

His youngest, cockiest, most annoying brother. A guy who claimed he was holding out for royalty every time anyone asked him why he always avoided serious relationships. As it stood, Miss Texas was about as close to royalty as you could get in the Lone Star State.

Which didn't explain why she was kissing him instead of Fox.

An incoming text buzzed on the phone inside Emerson's pocket. He slowly eased it from his pocket and gave his screen a discreet glance.

The message was from the King of Pranksters himself. It was short and to the point.

I see your dream gal has arrived. You're welcome, bro.

Emerson was more puzzled than ever. It sounded to him like Fox, who claimed to be holding out for royalty, had somehow pranked Lacey Perry into coming to plant a kiss on his next older brother. It didn't add up. His youngest brother never did anything without an agenda. He was up to something alright, and that was never a good thing.

EPILOGUE

June

Julia was amazed at how packed the Twin Canyons Park had remained for the entire first two months of the first racing season. It felt like a miracle, and she was more grateful than words could express. A series of miracles, actually.

Not only had her new business venture brought her family closer, it had also brought the entire town of Chipper closer. Lots of local business owners were benefitting from the influx of out-of-town riders and tourists. It was a win-win-win situation!

Today, the park was quickly filling up for a whole different reason. It was a Tuesday afternoon in June. There were no races scheduled for today. Instead, family and friends were gathering on the lush green turf in the center of the racetrack.

An enormous white tent had been erected beside the mini-lakes. Dozens of chairs were lined up in neat rows beneath it. A swatch of red rose petals lined the long aisle between the two sections of chairs.

Devlin Cassidy took his place at the front of the tent beneath a white-painted iron rose trellis. His brothers were standing on one side of him. His three sisters-in-law and two of Julia's friends were standing on the other side of him.

As the hired bluegrass violin and cello quartet plucked the opening notes of the wedding march, Julia gripped her father's arm.

"I'm getting married," she breathed, feeling faint. Her heart was racing faster than the horses that normally circled the racetrack.

"I'm so proud of you, kid." Cody Benson had a new straw Stetson perched jauntily on his sun-streaked hair. He'd traded in his jeans for an ivory tuxedo.

"I'm proud of you, too, Dad. And Mom. I love you both so much!" Julia's heart felt like it was bursting as he led her in the first sashaying step down the rose petal strewn pathway.

The lacy train of her gown rustled behind them. The water spouts gushed on the lake. Birds twittered from the trees and shrubs. The flowers edging the walkway outside the tent were heavy with blooms. It was the perfect day for a wedding.

Or two weddings, in their case.

As Julia made her way slowly toward her groom, their gazes caught and held. For a breathless moment, everyone else disappeared, and it was just the two of them alone in the tent. He was wearing a tuxedo the same shade as the one her father was wearing, though his brothers were wearing jeans beneath their matching ivory jackets. The brides-maids' dresses rustled like lilacs in the breeze as she finally reached his side.

There was a slight hesitation in Cody Benson's movements as he transferred his daughter's hand from his arm to Dev's arm. "Take care of her." It was as much of a warning as a commission.

"I will, sir." Dev's hand closed possessively over Julia's as he drew her closer to him.

Her father took his place on Julia's other side. The three of them faced the aisle together, waiting, as the wedding march continued to play longer than it normally would.

Brooke Flanagan appeared at the top of the aisle next, her gaze shimmering with happy tears. This day had come nearly twenty-seven years later than it should have, but it was finally here.

Her brother, Pete Flanagan, proudly took his place beside her and crooked his arm at her. His neck and hands were intricately tattooed, his face a maze of scars from his days as a champion bull rider. Like his sister, though, he was a survivor. He was also the president of the Circle of Hope, the organization he'd started to help his sister. There was a smattering of applause as the two of them began their march down the aisle.

Julia's eyes glistened with mirroring emotion as she watched her mother move forward to claim the happiness she'd waited so long for. The moment she arrived at the rose trellis, Cody Benson reached for her hands. A collective sigh rose from the audience at the look he gave his bride-to-be. Uncle Pete stepped back to take his place beside Dixie in the front row of guests. Then the two grooms and two brides turned in unison to face the minister.

A double wedding ceremony ensued, during which twice the normal number of promises and I-do's were exchanged. Twice the number of kisses were given to seal those promises, and a mother and daughter became married women on the same day at the same time on the same racetrack.

There were few dry eyes in the audience when the final prayer and blessings were given. The clapping and cheers went on and on afterward. Cameras flashed endlessly as family and friends strove to capture every last detail of the momentous occasion.

Dev leaned closer to Julia to quote what was fast becoming her favorite scripture as the two of them took their places in the receiving line. "Three things will last forever — faith, hope, and love — and the greatest of these is love."

She wrapped her hands around his arm, smiling joyously up at him. "I'm so happy, Dev!"

"I know the feeling, Mrs. Cassidy." He worshipped her with his eyes until the first guest enveloped them in a hug.

———

Like this book? Leave a review now!

Ready to find out if Emerson can make Miss Texas fall in love with the real him…and why Fox has pranked her into coming to town?
Check out
Mr. Yeah, Right. As If….

Much love,
Jo

SNEAK PREVIEW: MR. YEAH, RIGHT. AS IF...

A cowboy trying to get the woman of his dreams to fall in love with him before she figures out she's been pranked into dating him in this slightly mistaken identity romance...

Lacey Perry wears the Miss Texas crown for being a champion of humanitarian causes. When she finds out that a small town cowboy is secretly sending supplies to her favorite orphanage in Dallas, she decides to thank him for his generosity:

- With a surprise visit
- In person
- On his birthday

It's the kind of publicity stunt her social media followers are sure to love. Except she soon finds out it's not the only stunt in play. Between a missed flight, too many mixed signals to count, and an unexpected attraction, does her visit with Emerson stand a chance at turning into a real relationship? Or will her followers rate it as her worst dating disaster yet?

———

Grab your copy!
Mr. Yeah, Right. As If…

COWBOY CONFESSIONS
Read them all!
Mr. Not Right for Her
Mr. Maybe Right for Her
Mr. Right But She Doesn't Know It
Mr. Right Again for Her
Mr. Yeah, Right. As If…

Much love,
Jo

NOTE FROM JO

Don't worry! There's a lot more going on at Cassidy Farm, and you don't have to wait until the next book to read it.

Because...*drum roll*...I have some Bonus Content for

you. To access it, all you have to do is sign up for my mailing list. There will be a special bonus content for each COWBOY CONFESSIONS book, just for my subscribers. Also, you'll hear about my next new book as soon as it's out *(plus you get a free book)*. Woohoo!

As always, thank you for reading and loving my books!

JOIN CUPPA JO READERS!

If you're on Facebook, please join my group, Cuppa Jo Readers. Don't miss out on the giveaways + all the sweet and swoony cowboys!

https://www.facebook.com/groups/ CuppaJoReaders

GET A FREE BOOK!

Join my mailing list to be the first to know about new releases, free books, special discount prices, and other giveaways.

https://BookHip.com/JNNHTK

SNEAK PREVIEW: THE PLUS ONE RESCUE

TEXAS HOTLINE SERIES, BOOK #1

espite the center's no PDA rule, an instant attraction simmers between an expert search and rescue instructor and a broody firefighter during summer training.

Axel Hammerstone is lauded as a hometown hero when he returns from an overseas deployment with a Purple Heart and silver star. Nobody sees the inner scars of war he's still grappling with. As a tribute to the battle buddies who never made it home, he's determined to devote the rest of his career to search and rescue operations.

Kristi Kimiko is living her dream as an expert search and rescue instructor at the Texas Hotline Training Center. Unfortunately, it leaves her little time for dating. When the hunky Axel half-limps and half-swaggers into her renowned dog training course with his beautiful golden retriever, she is immediately drawn to him — and soon finds herself serving as his plus one at a family birthday celebration.

features. He'd come straight from the district office in his business suit, but his straw Stetson and leather boots underscored the fact that he was and always would be a rancher first. "Her return is nothing short of a miracle."

By a miracle, Josh knew Mr. Remington was referring to the fact that he'd negotiated long and hard with his fellow school board members to tweak a few of the job requirements in her favor. He'd wanted to hire a hometown girl as the next head principal of Heart Lake High, but Hope wouldn't have stood a chance in the interview if the powers-that-be hadn't waived the prior experience requirement. The ink was still drying on her PhD, and she'd only served as an assistant principal so far. This was the first time she would be running an entire high school on her own.

Josh was concerned about how much responsibility the school board was placing on her shoulders this early in her career. However, no one had asked for his opinion on the matter, so he was keeping it to himself. For now.

He was simply the guy they'd hired to protect her — off the record, of course. On paper, his security team was actually under contract to guard the student body and school facilities as a whole. Not one person, specifically. The sidebar agreement for Josh to stick as close to Hope as a cocklebur had happened in a closed-door meeting with the superintendent, alone. Though the older gentleman was only distantly related to Hope — a cousin of her grandparents twice removed — he'd always considered her to be family.

The door to the gleaming white Gulfstream opened, and a set of equally gleaming white metal stairs descended. A red high-heeled boot appeared next. It was soon followed by the rest of the woman Josh had waited so long to see again. Her long, blonde hair was draped over one shoulder, cascading nearly to the waist of her sassy denim dress. She wasn't as tanned as she used to be, probably because of the number of hours she was required to spend indoors these days. But she still had her impetuous smile and walked with the same energy and confidence of the barrel racing, rodeo queen he remembered.

Though Josh didn't so much as flinch, it felt like a sucker punch in the gut to watch Hope Remington walk down the jet stairs and move across the pavement to the airline terminal. Toward him, instead of away from him, for the first time in ten years.

Only a single wall of glass separated them now. He and the district superintendent had been awaiting her arrival from the other side of it. Though Josh sorely doubted Hope would appreciate his presence, Mr. Remington had insisted he be included in her welcome party. Then again, she'd moved on with her life years ago. Maybe she'd long since forgiven and forgotten his past sins. There was a distinct possibility she wouldn't even recognize the older version of him. He was a good four inches taller than the last time they'd been together — bigger, broader, and wiser. *Infinitely* wiser. A man who'd learned from his mistakes and had no interest in repeating them.

There was no way she'd be feeling even half of what he was feeling when she finally laid eyes on him and realized who he was — pain laced with bitter longing over the way he'd left things between them. Of all the things he'd left unsaid and even worse, the things he'd left undone. Especially the way he'd failed to meet her at their favorite rendezvous and run off to college together, like the lovesick fools they'd once been.

She'd been a slender teenager at the time, full of dreams and plans that were bigger than him, anxious to leave their small town existence behind and explore the world in ways only a Remington could afford to do. She was a grown woman with big city polish now, one who'd tasted and experienced the globe from Anchorage, to Amsterdam, to Paris. Yeah, he'd followed her adventures by lurking on her social media accounts, since she'd never bothered kicking him off. His lurking had also kept him painfully informed about her social life. There'd been pictures of all the places she'd visited and all the friends she'd made along the way. Guy friends. Lots of guy friends. He wondered how many of them she'd dated.

Those pictures were the only reason Josh knew that the auburn-haired man striding at her side in a designer gray suit was more than her pilot. He was one of her closest friends, possibly her boyfriend. A billionaire philanthropist from Alaska, who was supposedly coming to help clear the tornado damage in Heart Lake by financing a number of their restoration projects — the first and biggest project being the overhaul of their disaster planning and preparedness infrastructure.

But Josh wasn't buying the guy's story. He could think of only one reason why a man of Kellan Maddox's elite connections and financial resources would travel to such a small, rural town, and that was to pursue the heart of the woman Josh had never stopped loving.

Well, Mr. Money Bags was in for one heck of a surprise when he discovered the competition he would be going up against.

Me.

Josh pulled his Stetson low over his eyes as the gate door flew open, and Hope stepped inside the terminal. He preferred not to be recognized right away. He'd rather witness her unrehearsed reaction to the sight of him when she finally realized who he was.

Her expressive blue gaze scanned the small waiting area and quickly lit on Mr. Remington.

"Elmer!" she cried joyfully.

Josh experienced a familiar jolt at the sound of her voice. It was all he could do not to step forward and sweep her into his arms as she moved in their direction. She hurried forward with her hands outstretched. Not to him, unfortunately.

Mr. Remington eagerly took her slender hands in his. "Welcome home, Hope." He leaned in to kiss her cheek. "We couldn't be happier that you've agreed to join our staff at Heart Lake High."

She gave his wrinkled hands an affectionate squeeze back before dropping them. "How could I say no to such a kind and generous offer? There certainly aren't many twenty-nine-year-old administrators out there getting this kind of opportunity handed to them."

The superintendent nodded sagely.

Her smile widened to a full blast of warmth and humor. "I probably don't want to know how many arms you twisted or favors you called in to make this happen."

"You're the right person for the job, Hope," he assured quickly. "Don't you ever doubt it. It's the only reason I reached out and asked you to apply."

"I'm so glad you did," she murmured. Her smile dimmed a few degrees, as her gaze became washed with nostalgia. "As soon as I heard about the storm damage, I knew I needed to come home."

"Don't thank me yet." Mr. Remington grimaced. "Combining two high school campuses isn't exactly going to be a stroll around the lake."

"I understand what needs to be done, sir." She met his gaze soberly. "That's why it had to be me, isn't it?"

"Yes."

Josh knew what they were leaving unsaid. Hope was a hometown girl. An insider, despite all the years she'd been gone. She was one of the few people in the county who stood a chance at maneuvering her way through the politics, family feuds, and old grudges that fueled everything that took place in their small mountain town. She'd grown up in the middle of those politics. She'd been an integral part of them. Only time would tell how much of them remained in her, how they would fuel her plans and drive her decisions.

Elmer Remington and his school board were banking on the fact that her decisions in the coming days would drive their high school in the right direction, toward a unity that the students from the north and south sides of town had never before tasted. They'd been arch rivals for years. Putting them under one roof for the first time was a lofty goal at best, a foolish one at worst.

In that moment, Hope's natty airline pilot strode over to join their group. Up until now, he'd been conferring with the gate attendant, signing paperwork and such. He held out a hand to the superintendent. "I'm Kellan Maddox. You must be the Elmer Remington I've heard so much about."

Josh's upper lip curled at the ruby signet ring riding the man's pinky finger, along with the diamonds glinting from his cufflinks. *What a pretty boy!* If this was the kind of man that revved Hope's motor these days, then she'd changed in ways Josh had never considered her capable of changing. Lifting his jaw a fraction, he drilled her with a curious stare while the two men shook hands.

Without preamble, Mr. Remington dropped Pretty Boy's hand and turned in Josh's direction. "Hope, I

ALSO BY JO GRAFFORD

For the most up-to-date printable list of my books:

Click here

or go to:

https://www.JoGrafford.com/books

For the most up-to-date printable list of books by Jo
Grafford, writing as Jovie Grace *(sweet historical romance)*:

Click here

or go to:

https://www.jografford.com/joviegracebooks

ABOUT JO

Jo is an Amazon bestselling author of sweet and inspirational romance stories about faith, hope, love and family drama with a few Texas-sized detours into comedy.

1.) Follow on Amazon!
amazon.com/author/jografford

2.) Join Cuppa Jo Readers!
https://www.facebook.com/groups/
CuppaJoReaders

3.) Follow on Bookbub!
https://www.bookbub.com/authors/jo-grafford

4.) Follow on YouTube

https://www.youtube.com/channel/
UC3R1at97Qso6BXiBIxCjQ5w

a amazon.com/authors/jo-grafford
BB bookbub.com/authors/jo-grafford
f facebook.com/jografford

Made in United States
North Haven, CT
20 October 2023

42988652R00136